Cheyney's Law

Colonel Allen Cheyney is shaped in the mould of predecessors who are household names in the fictional world of Clubland Heroes.

Cheyney *'had refused all decorations and honours, including the V.C. and a knighthood ... He had unmasked Philby, though it had taken him years ... to do it; and he had killed Philby's spymaster, Markham, missing the servant by hours in Beirut. He kept a dog, and a flat, and was restoring a ruined house in Scotland.'*

Here, in his first recorded adventure, Cheyney is called on to help a friend whose son has vanished. And in vanishing Tommy had left behind a very distinctive black octagonal badge which was of particular interest to Superintendent Pierce of the Metropolitan C.I.D. Scotland Yard had seen some of these badges before, but only in the possession of master crooks and terrorists. How had one come into the possession of young Tommy Graham?

Soon the action becomes fast and furious. Cheyney and Pierce find themselves in deadly trouble. One escape only leads to another capture – and in the end Cheyney finds himself fighting alone against a gang headed by a man bent on evil and wickedness, crazed with power, greed and hatred.

There are many scenes of violence – in country houses, in shady London clubs, and on the west coast of Scotland when the dénouement finally comes.

This splendid first thriller by a scholar and journalist represents something different and unfashionable in the current phase of the crime novel. It may be said defiantly to recall some of the great styles and traditions of this branch of literature, while successfully adapting them to the modern scene and providing a diet of sustained excitement.

by the same author

Non-Fiction

CHEYNEY'S LAW

PATRICK COSGRAVE

M

© Patrick Cosgrave 1977

ISBN: 0 333 21635 0

First published 1977 by
MACMILLAN LONDON LIMITED
London and Basingstoke
Associated companies in New York
Dublin Melbourne Johannesburg and Delhi

Printed in Great Britain by
FLETCHER AND SON LIMITED
Norwich
and bound by
RICHARD CLAY (THE CHAUCER PRESS) LIMITED
Bungay, Suffolk

For George Hardinge

CONTENTS

CHAPTER ONE

An Old Friend

He arrived at eight, never spoke before nine, when he was given his first cup of coffee, and never received telephone calls after noon. Not only did he not receive calls, he did not want to know they had been made; so the diplomacy surrounding them lay entirely within Miss Levison's province. However, the essence of genius in a secretary is to know – or guess – when the rules should be broken.

Miss Levison laid the notes she was carrying on the small corner table which served Cheyney as a place for drinks, poured him a glass of dry sherry, and carried sherry and papers over to his desk. He thanked her, and she said, 'There was a telephone call.' He looked up.

Cheyney is about fifty, lean and hard and bony. He has an angular Scottish face and a cropped but untidy head of hair of that impossible mixture of colours between fair and grey which only the Scots seem able to achieve. It is the only untidy thing about him: for the rest, he is impeccably conservative, from the tiny knot of his regimental tie within its hard collar through the pinstripe suit to the dully shining black shoes. There were other and quite different Cheyneys, but in Westminster there was only this one, the feared and perplexing Colonel the Hon. Allen Cheyney, immured in the fortress of his own personality, arrogant, undefiled and ruthless.

This was Cheyney who had refused all decorations and honours, including the V.C. and the knighthood to which length of service by itself entitled him. This was Cheyney who had seen Richmond on to a train at Zagreb and who had brought the American Sam Geary back from behind the lines in Korea. He had unmasked Philby, though it had taken him years, and one of his several resignations, to do it; and he had killed Philby's spymaster, Markham, missing the servant by hours in Beirut. He kept a dog, and a flat, and was restoring a ruined house in Scotland. He had no other known vices.

'What?'

Miss Levison had no clear idea why she had mentioned this particular call. She had broken Cheyney's rule only once before in three years – when Richmond had called from Belgrade – and now she was confused, and felt her heart turning over. He held the paper he was reading in his left hand and drummed gently with the fingers of his right on the bare desk, looking at her and waiting.

'He said his name was Peter Graham, sir. And he said, to tell you he needed you.'

He looked down.

'Did he leave a number?'

'Yes, sir.'

Miss Levison began to feel she had done right. Sensing her feeling Cheyney looked up and smiled.

'Ring him back, please. Tell him I will lunch with him at the Arches at half-past one.'

Miss Levison was now in a turmoil. Like any other man of business Colonel Cheyney occasionally cancelled lunches at short notice. But, as a good secretary, she knew the people for whom he cancelled and the people who were cancellable. The name of Peter Graham did not appear on the first list.

'Colonel,' she said – only at moments of real stress did she call him that – 'General Smith.'

'You will have to put him off.'

Like most men Cheyney had no idea of the burdens imposed on a secretary by his simple instructions. A battle royal with at least the other man's secretary was certain: in this case it would be even worse, since the Director of the Joint Warfare Establishment would long since have left Miss Simpson's area of protection, and might already be at the Carlton. Not for the first time Miss Levison felt her employer was not to be borne with.

Cheyney, handing her back the notes she had placed on his desk, was making the burden even heavier.

'I cannot say when I can see Smith. Perhaps tomorrow. Give them my apologies.'

He took half his glass of sherry in a swallow and stood up.

'Thank you Miss Levison. Call my car, please, for a quarter-past.'

Miss Levison left and Cheyney went to look out of the window.

Three-quarters of an hour later Cheyney arrived at the Arches. It is a peculiar club, taking its name from the architecture surrounding the stone steps leading down to its entrance, and its membership is exclusive if not, with any certainty, respectable. Cheyney was well-known there, but no guest, arriving in advance of his host, was allowed to proceed beyond the miserable and drinkless entry lobby. Guests, indeed, were frowned upon: they could be entertained neither in the bar nor in the dining-room, and were confined to one of the half-dozen cells called private rooms. The service in these was slow, and the food plain. Trays of drinks were laid out in each cell, though the member who asked for something not provided – or who sought *more* than was provided – could whistle for his pains. The Arches is a monument to the preference of the British male for fellowship at the expense of comfort: but it is rare for more than two of the six private rooms to be in use at any one time.

Cheyney and Graham met upstairs briefly. Now, having been offered a choice between mutton and beef and having both chosen beef, they looked at one another across a deal table and two large Scotches. They had not seen one another for five years, though Graham, having retired from the Navy, had been back in England for two. Their friendship had been less formed than cemented when Graham, in a cutter from a ship, the command of which was far below his rank, had taken Cheyney off the coast of China during the Quemoy affair. They rarely met, never reminisced, scarcely spoke. But one would have gone to Patagonia at the request of the other.

They were, recognisably, men of the same stamp. But, while Cheyney had clearly held to the vocation, Graham, equally clearly, had relaxed his grip. He was still a powerful man. But middle age could be seen in the thick, shiny and useless flesh on the backs of his hands. His waistcoat rose a little above the waist of his trousers, and his cheeks had started to go veiny. The fat had not yet eaten into him, for his ability had won him success in business since he had left the Navy. His experience and intelligence were frequently called on, especially in the design and production of oil rig supply ships which needed to lie as low in the water as was compatible with heavy loads, to be inexpensive in construction, fast in passage, and cheaper to use than the ships of the competition. Graham was well-to-do now, and richer by far than he would have been if he had served out his time in the Navy.

All this was in Cheyney's mind after ten minutes of talk. Graham would never lose the tan burned into his broken skin by years at sea, nor could his voice ever forfeit an officer's rasp. Yet, there was some uncertainty about him now that could not be put down to relaxed living. Cheyney had enough self-awareness to know that he was himself an impossibly monkish man, a condition which had advantages as well as disadvantages. But there had been challenges in his life from which he had shrunk: swimming from the Chinese coast to Hong Kong after, fit though he was, he had been beaten and starved, was one such. He had told himself he could do it; and in bitter self-reprisal reminded himself of the hundreds of wretches who, escaping from Mao's frugal paradise, did it every week – some drowning, some surviving, some, nowadays, being sent back by a brutal government – when Peter Graham, two hours behind schedule, but making a perfect landfall, crept up to a shivering and chattering Cheyney in the dark and, in that whisper that was like a roar, said, 'What-ho, old boy.' Cheyney had cursed him and told him to keep his voice down. Afterwards, they had got terribly drunk on neat rum.

Although Graham and Cheyney had never reminisced it was clear that, on this occasion, reminiscence would be the bridge between what Graham wanted to say and his saying it. During a pause in talk he went to the sideboard, replenished their glasses and said:

'How are your lot now?'

'Oh, so-so.'

'Richmond. What about him? Bright lad.'

'Oh, left us.'

'Oh.'

Then they sat for a bit, twiddling and pretending to savour drink, passing the odd comment one to another as though there was nothing more natural than a lunch in the Arches between Rear-Admiral Sir Peter Graham and Colonel Cheyney. The waiter came and fed them, placed a carafe of claret between them and went away. Affection flowed between them; and so did doubt and hesitancy. Cheyney said:

'Do you miss the Navy?'

'Well, it's very computerised now, you know. A ship of

war isn't something you sail – it's something you manage.'

'But you must be pleased to be home.'

'Oh yes.'

'And well off. You can do things you want to.'

'Oh yes.'

The tension vibrated in the air between the two men. Something should be said, something had to justify Graham's telephone call to Cheyney. Cheyney, whose forte was decision, felt the pressure of the conversation beat inside his head like drums. Everything told him to ask: but he could not. He could see – for he was an acute man – the misery in Peter Graham's face. But he could not ask. He owed his friend that much.

The waiter came and cleared the plates away. It was a release and an excuse for, clearly, they could not talk when he was present. Appalled in his inner mind Cheyney heard himself ask Graham about the weather in Britain compared to that in the Far East and, even more appalled, heard Graham reply.

The waiter laid out cheese; and poured coffee; and went away. There was a great pause. And then Graham said:

'Allen, it's my son.'

Then he told the story that had begun three months before.

CHAPTER TWO

Peter Graham's Story

When we got back from the East Tommy was eighteen. He had been to school in England, of course, but a lot of his holiday time was spent abroad, nearly always with Maria and myself. (We visited England at least once a year, but for the last ten years we had spent holidays all over the place: we were going to settle at home when I retired, and never move far again; so we thought we'd get all the travel in first.)

Anyway, Tommy had had a completely free year after school and he was going up to Cambridge. The year was spent in Australia. He was, we reckoned, a good boy, but then I've found that a lot of Service youngsters who spend a lot of time on station don't seem to be affected with the same kind of bug as the children at home. He has Maria's colouring, you know, not mine. He's as blond as brass and has her blue eyes and her figure – he's taller than I am now. He is good at games in a slapdash kind of way – fair bat, swims well, boxes pretty well. He's not exactly a bookish boy, but he was always good at his books, if you see what I mean. He'd get a good degree, I think, maybe even a first if he really wanted it and worked hard. History was his subject. He hasn't wanted to be a sailor since he was a child, about fifteen. I must say I haven't encouraged him. It doesn't have a great deal of meaning for a lad now, not in this climate, not with economics and politicians today. There's not likely to be any fighting that's important.

That's why I planned to get out early – I found a job before I left – and got together the kind of nest egg that would be better than a pension. We bought the house in Kent three years before I left the Navy – pretty confident, we were, that I'd get a job – and spent a lot of money on it. It's a decent size, eight or so bedrooms and about ten acres of land to play with. I always take Friday off unless I'm up North, so I get three clear days to work on it.

You'll think I'm getting away from Tommy, but I'm not. You've got to understand the kind of life we were trying to build. I'd seen the end coming in the Navy for a long time – not for me, I was safe enough, could have gone higher – but for the thing. God, I was bitter at first. When I thought that there was never going to be anything for me to do again, I mean – me the country, not just the Service. But I thought about it and Maria and I talked for ages. We used to sit there in the evening with rum punches and watch the sun going, and go inside only when it got really cold and get sozzled. You know how much cleverer you are, when you're pissed. It was like that.

But we started to put the bits together all right. It really was like a jigsaw – no, it was like building a wall (I've been building a wall at home), slow and careful and uncertain. But we got it up all right, we got it up. We were very philosophical in the end – sorry, did I say that before? We were very philosophical. Thanks.

What was I saying? Oh yes. We made a plan. We decided to spend as much time as we could going to all the old places, getting ready to go back to a burrow, in England. It's not always so good, going back, but sometimes it's very good. Even the sadness – you get to feel you can't do without it.

Anyway, Tommy went up to Cambridge, I got busy with oil, and I even played with writing a book – naval history, you know, nothing political. Maria got back to painting, and she did all sorts of other things. The first year went pretty well. I don't mind telling you I wasn't bursting with joy over some of Tommy's things. It wasn't that he was going Red. But he started getting untidy – jeans and long hair and so on. And he gave up sports pretty completely, except squash, which he played a lot of, so he was pretty fit. I thought the year down under would have stopped him being fanciful, like the undergraduates you hear about – and he wasn't bad, you understand – and I hadn't been a very disciplined boy myself. So I kept quiet about the things I didn't like, and I tried to be tolerant. He seemed to be getting on well with Maria, so I didn't worry too much. Well, maybe I was a bit eager. If he was home for the occasional weekend, or on holidays, I was terribly bucked if he joined me in the garden, and I'm afraid I said so. I was a bit down when his prelims were only fair, and not too pleased that he seemed to have absolutely no idea what he wanted to do, especially as he seemed to be losing all his old interests. I found him one day reading a book by Marx – *Grundrisse*, it was – and I made some joke about it. 'Oh, father,' he said, 'it's very important.'

That was the first year. This one has gone to hell. What? Yes, please. Scotch.

Tommy's hair got longer, for one thing. And he came to see us less often in term time. When he did he was bloody surly – I tell you that. And then we had Sunday week last. The copper came.

I'm sorry. I thought of him just like that. The bell rang and I opened the door and I saw him and I knew he was bad news. I knew, Allen, that the boy had done something stupid. It had been building up inside my head. *I knew it.* I remember looking past Inspector Smith – the copper – at my garden, my trees, my son. It was a nice Spring night, y'know. I didn't say, 'What are you here for?' I said, 'Come in.'

Heavy. That's the thing I remember about the Inspector. He was a heavy man; and he had a heavy manner. Thanks. Yeh. I think I can remember precisely what he said, Allen. He said: 'We've got your boy at the station, sir – drugs, sir – I'm afraid.' Once he said it I knew he was right. I didn't understand, you know, but I knew he was right.

Well, look Allen, I don't want to bore you. Maria got hysterical, but we went down to the station and bailed Tommy out. It was bloody ghastly, I tell you. Honestly, Allen, it was. I paid the bail and it was ghastly. Did you know police stations smelt of sawdust?

You probably do. Yeh. Thanks. Anyway, we came back with Tommy, Maria crying, and all that. I gave Tommy a row in my study and he just sulked. Sulked, Allen. Just bloody sulked. Next morning he wasn't there.

I got up at five as usual. I walked around and lost my temper with Tommy. It was so glorious, my patch, my daffodils, my walk, my fish-pond. I promise, Allen, that I breathed in that special air – that *home* air – and decided to forgive him. And then, when I got back to the house I found the little bugger had gone. And, Allen, I found these.

Cheyney looked down at the detritus of a teenage life.

CHAPTER THREE

Superintendent Pierce

Detective Chief Superintendent Pierce was a man of granite. He was neither tall nor bulky, but his impassivity had about it some unbroken quality. Yet, the more one studied him the less clear one was about the source of his strength: his face was almost featureless, and his fair eyebrows practically non-existent. He dressed in light tweeds; his hair was thinning; his hands square and spatulate. Perhaps, thought Cheyney, sitting across from him in a high and airless office in New Scotland Yard, it was that Pierce created unease in any interlocutor by his unnatural stillness. His only marked nervous characteristic was his intolerance of paper on his desk when he was speaking to anybody. And when Cheyney had been shown in, as always happened, the few bits and pieces that Pierce was studying were instantly swept into the centre drawer. Now Pierce sat in perfect stillness, his fingers looped loosely together over his stomach, gazing impassively at the pathetic collection of objects Cheyney had taken from Peter Graham.

'So,' said Cheyney, 'it's not the drugs that seized my attention immediately, it's the black badge.'

'Yes,' said Pierce, but without nodding. Another man would have picked up again the octagonal black piece of plastic which Cheyney had brought him. Pierce merely went on looking at it.

Without shifting his position Pierce began to speak, slowly and precisely, in his featureless voice. He would be a formidable interrogator, Cheyney thought – that was, indeed, his reputation, but Cheyney had never seen him in action – for the dry coldness of his voice froze the still air in the room around them and could easily be fancied to have built up an atmosphere of fear. This was all the more so because Pierce made it plain that he was himself a worried man.

'I don't mind telling you, Cheyney,' said Pierce, 'that I am more worried and foxed than I've ever been in my life. I would feel we were getting somewhere if I could even guess whether this thing was political or just commercial. Let me see. This is the fourth of these things we've come across. The first one we took from Grey, and he was a senior thug and went down for life. The second we got from that bunch of anarchists that bloody judge sent down for a couple of years apiece, just because their damned bomb hadn't hurt anybody. And the third was concealed in that Birmingham house where we found a million in heroin. The point about each of those occasions was that a major enterprise of some sort was involved, and the people concerned were in every case senior in their various misbegotten enterprises. If the badges are what we've always thought they were – some kind of identification for high-ups – how the devil could one come into the possession of an undergraduate running away from home?; and how in heaven's name could the boy have come to leave them behind? You didn't know this boy?'

Cheyney shook his head. 'Not since he was just a kid. I've repeated to you exactly what his father told me; and that Peter Graham is a very old friend.'

'Tell me about the effect this had on him again?'

'He's very cut up. But why are you so interested in him?'

'I don't know. I'm casting about. For instance. You say Graham is quite an important man in his own line of business, and he may well still have useful Naval connections. I'm hanged if I know, we're checking. If the boy was some sort of spy on his father and then decided he couldn't take it and did a bunk, he might have left that badge behind, either in a panic or as some sort of warning.'

Cheyney considered it. 'It's theoretically plausible. But I doubt if Peter Graham is that important. If the guess we've worked on for the past six months has been right and those badges are a mark of the presence of pretty high-powered people in this gang, then I can see no way that Peter Graham would be important enough to have somebody of that calibre working on him. Have you considered the possibility that young Tommy had got in on the fringes of this organisation, somehow got hold of a card, and was then spirited away?'

'I don't see it. Certainly, they're not as efficient as we might have feared. But, then, they can hardly be, since they obviously employ all sorts of fringe figures in the crime and drugs world. But they're still bloody efficient. We know, or guess, who they've been behind and what, and there still isn't a whisper of importance from any of our sources: they've got the underworld as baffled – or scared – as they have us.'

'There must be a factor we're missing.'

The two men sat in silence for a few moments. For weeks now, they had been meeting just the same impasse, and for weeks these silences had fallen between them. Cheyney took out his case and lit a cigarette, noting, but affecting not to, the disapproval that wafted from the man across the desk, a disapproval that Pierce seemed able to convey in spite of neither moving a muscle nor letting any expression appear in his eyes. 'Let's have Graham in,' said Cheyney, wondering how Pierce would convey a signal without moving.

Apparently he had a footbell, for a moment later a young policewoman brought Peter Graham in to join them. Since lunch he had become genuinely haggard for, though

Cheyney had told him nothing of consequence, he was realist enough to know that something more significant was going on than the search for a missing son of a friend, even if the boy had been on drugs. His face had crumpled, his skin gone dry, and his hands were twitching. A sharp look of mingled pain and fear came into his eyes when he looked at the pile of his son's undesirable possessions on Pierce's uncluttered desk. Without rudeness, but also without greeting, Pierce gave the barest of nods to Cheyney, who turned to his old friend and spoke gently.

'Peter, I haven't been at all frank with you. But Superintendent Pierce agrees with me that you should know what we believe we are up against. Tommy's disappearance, or at least whatever he has been up to, is closely connected with a much bigger show.'

Cheyney's face became leaner and harder and his eyes frostier as, looking right at his old friend, he went on talking.

'About six months ago my department got on the track of a man called Oldfield, an Army Sergeant. He wasn't a major espionage operative himself, but he was, for a very brief period, in a position to do a great deal of harm. He was certain to be discovered, but his employers and he clearly thought that capture was a risk he had to run for the sake of taking what was available to him over a matter of a few days. We took him – I did it myself – but we lost the stuff. Now, as you know, most intelligence services will try to spring agents who have run the kind of risk Oldfield ran, and the police were especially careful of him. It made no difference. There was a vicious ambush and Oldfield vanished. Two policemen were killed, and three crippled. We've had a sufficient number of espionage scandals, and we managed to keep it quiet that this raid had anything to do with spies. Moreover, Pierce and his men were convinced that the ambush to free Oldfield was not the work of any intelligence service's hit men, but of straightforward criminals.'

Cheyney paused as his mind assembled the next stage of his narrative, and Admiral Graham licked very dry lips and hawked as though there was no spittle in his mouth.

'By a series of extraordinary breaks we were able to connect the ambush with a man called Clement Grey, who was described by Pierce a moment ago as a senior thug. That is exactly what he was – one of perhaps the top half-dozen gunmen available to British criminal bosses, and nearly as good as the top Americans. We took Grey and he went down for life. There is no chance of making him talk, for the prosecution made it clear that a blunder within his own organisation was what set us on his track, so he could not feel he had been betrayed by his bosses. But my own belief is that, knowing the way the police go after people who kill policemen, whoever employed Grey sent him over. Where Oldfield is I have no idea. Now, any connection between the criminal classes and foreign espionage is of instant and major concern both to myself and to the police, so Pierce here and I set up a small joint task force to go into the business. The only thing that remotely resembled a clue – and that only because we could not understand it – was a plastic octagonal badge found in Grey's possession which was exactly identical to the one in Tommy's room.'

He tapped the piece of plastic on the desk, which was marked only by an embossed capital 'Q' in the centre, and paused.

Peter Graham looked as though he had been shot. He started forward and then almost doubled up in his chair. His prominent eyes bulged and he reached a hand to his collar as though he were choking.

In a conversation like this one Cheyney took his mind out of his head, away from his emotions, and imagined it floating, disembodied, somewhere above him. If he was gentle, or concerned, or angry, or threatening, it was a function of that separate thing in the air: only that way could he interrogate, every feeling a function of his purpose. Now, however, it was as though, after all, strings attached the mind to the heart. He had never conceived that, under whatever pressure, Graham could break like that: it had never been in the man. But Graham had broken, and Cheyney's strings remained. So he went on, still speaking unemotionally, but now with more pace, as though to get it over.

'Between Grey and Tommy we found two more such badges. The first was in a house lived in by the anarchist bombers known as the Wild Bunch, whom we took a few days after Grey, and the second was in a Birmingham house raided – successfully – for drugs ten days ago. We have been able to get nothing from any of the possessors of any one of them, and the best interrogators in both the police and my department are convinced that, if any of our prisoners really know what these things are, they are too terrified to tell. Let me just add one thing more...'

Graham interrupted. 'Drink,' he got out.

Cheyney paused and Pierce rose slowly, though not lethargically, from behind his desk and went to a cupboard. He returned in a moment with a bottle of whisky, a glass and a carafe of water. For Graham he poured a very stiff whisky. Graham added a little water, and took a swallow. It was impossible that his face could go pale, but a greyness suffused his tan, and he looked eighty. He fumbled for a cigarette and Cheyney lit one for him. He looked as though he was going to say something, could not get whatever it was out and just nodded desperately to Cheyney. He was a man in the deepest of shock, and he was broken apart.

'One thing more,' continued Cheyney, 'in all cases like

this there are a whole series of indicators I and the police can use to pick up hints and clues. We are convinced, on a mass of evidence, but not anything we could go into court with, that these three incidents which we have been able definitely to connect are only parts of something very much larger. Understand, we have nothing hard and mathematical which enables us to say this; nor do we know whether the mainspring of the whole thing is political or criminal. And, until we talked today we had nothing outside the pattern connecting each discovery of one of these badges or whatever they are with a serious crime or a serious criminal. Tommy breaks the pattern and, though I can't see why just now, he is important for that reason. But I must tell you that I am no longer just doing a favour for an old friend.'

There was then a protracted silence between the three men. Pierce fell into one of his rapt silences: it was as though he was no longer in the room. Graham stared, blank and broken, straight ahead of him. Only Cheyney seemed vibrant: his presence filled the room, and he seemed to be discharging energy to his own friend. He scarcely moved, save to light another cigarette and, this between his fingers, leant slightly towards Graham. His face seemed to take on colour, and his blue eyes glowed with some intangible force. Slowly Graham began to put the pieces of himself together: like a man who was drunk, but needed to sober up for something, he flexed his hands and stiffened his legs, testing and stretching his muscles and his reflexes. He tried to find his voice and, on the second attempt, succeeded.

'What can I do?'

Cheyney, who had been dreadfully tense, relaxed, and nodded at Pierce.

That strange man inclined himself forward slightly in his chair, and put his loosely linked hands together on the desk.

25

'From now on, Sir Peter, everything we say will be recorded. I am going to examine you very closely on the subject of your son, his background, his associations and his habits. Many of the questions will seem to be – will, indeed, be – trivial. But I have no real clue to go on. On the face of it, there would seem no likelihood of a connection between your son and Clement Grey, though the anarchists or the drug traffickers might provide us with a connection. But I want to find out everything I can and if, when you have left here, something else occurs to you – however irrelevant – whether it is something as unimportant as the fact that your boy liked processed peas, I want you to let me know it. Will you do all that?'

Graham paused and nodded, but he wanted to say something first.

'Superintendent, Allen – I don't know how I'm taking this. I'd like to say that you will have my full co-operation. But I loved that boy, and even now I cannot believe he was really bad. *Is* really bad. I don't know whether I might not cover for him, later. You'd better get everything out of me that you can before I put my nerves in a piece again.'

Pierce nodded and slowly, unemphatically, precisely, went about the business of putting together everything the father had known about the son. He cross-questioned Graham for more than two hours, spending endless time on Tommy's sporting proclivities, his slow drift away from parental companionship, and he was left at the end, as the evening shadows began to fill the office, with a meagre crop – little, in fact, more than Cheyney had garnered from Graham's story at lunch. By the end, it was clear that Graham was exhausted: his words were coming in broken spurts, tears were very near his eyes, and his tone was faint. Cheyney had tired, and got up several times to gaze out of the window. Only the imperturbable Pierce went on, untiring, indeed inexhaustible. Finally, however, even he drew to a close.

'I think, Sir Peter, we have gone as far as we can go. Have you a car?'

'Yes, but I don't want to drive home.'

'I will send a car with you. You realise, do you not, that we have only begun, that I will have to examine your house, cross question your wife? Will she be able to bear it?'

Graham nodded, past that point of exhaustion beyond which he was capable even of reflex. Then Pierce sent for a car for him and Cheyney took him down to the courtyard. He felt miserably helpless, and could manage only an ineffective pat on Graham's shoulder before the car drove away and he returned to Pierce's office.

He was himself tired, and hungry and thirsty. His mind was spinning with all the seemingly unconnected bits and pieces that Pierce's skilled questioning had extracted from the stricken father – but, unfortunately, extracted without providing either a pattern or a clue. He felt they had got precisely nowhere. He would need time to brood on what they had, to go over and over it again in his mind, seeking the one oddity, the one unusual thing that would provide a starting point.

When he rejoined Pierce the Superintendent was sitting exactly as Cheyney had left him. He knew from past experience of these lengthy sessions that it was useless to suggest dinner to Pierce who, on such occasions, merely shook his head slowly and remained looking at nothing. Cheyney, who was a man very sure of himself, and very confident, felt his own reputation dissolve somewhat in the presence of this remote creature, who seemed to survive without connections, without home, without even habits, and to live solely, brooding in this dreary office.

'Anything?'

27

'I can't see anything,' said Pierce, and the telephone rang.

He picked it up and waited. Then he uttered one word, 'When?'

'I'm coming,' he said, replaced the receiver and looked at Cheyney.

'Clement Grey escaped from prison an hour ago.'

CHAPTER FOUR

Clues and Diversions

The following morning Cheyney sat alone in the little breakfast room of his flat, pushed the breakfast things away from him, and began to try to think.

It was a dank and gloomy morning, and the increasing patter of the rain outside suggested sleet later in the day. However tired he was, and however late he had been the night before, Cheyney walked his Irish wolfhound, Bruce, at six o'clock in the morning. But there had been no pleasure in their stroll this morning, and Bruce had had to be towelled vigorously when Cheyney returned, irritable, puzzled and tired. He always cooked his own breakfast, the rest of his housekeeping chores – as well as others of a quite different nature – being attended to by Nelson, the enormous caretaker of the small block of flats in which he lived. He had to confess to himself that he could see no light whatever in the case which confronted him, and he longed for younger days when he had been a technical operative in the field, with simple and straightforward tasks to perform.

He had reached home at nearly three o'clock that morning, after fruitless hours spent with Pierce at Grey's prison, puzzling over the problem of how so dangerous a prisoner had been able to procure a gun, reach a roof, and escape to a waiting vehicle (they had no idea what it was) on the other side of the wall. Grey, the flustered and troubled governor had confessed, had been a surly but quite tractable inmate. He had not mixed with other prisoners, but he had obeyed regulations reasonably well and had received no visitors. Pierce and Cheyney were concerned with only one inquiry, only one point to which they returned again and again – was there any indication of whether the Grey rescue had been organised by his own criminal friends or by other hands? They were back, in other words, with a facet of the same question that had been puzzling them for six months – were they dealing with an enemy essentially political or essentially criminal – commercial, as Pierce put it?

And they were no nearer an answer. Cheyney got up and paced around his flat, the dog padding quietly behind him. It was an unpretentiously comfortable place, full of possessions scattered about, all suggesting a personality at once bookish and active. When Cheyney fiddled restlessly with the collection of walking sticks in the entrance hall Bruce whined and his master snapped at him. Then Cheyney went back to the little kitchen to make coffee and to try to examine the proposition which continually nagged at him that Tommy Graham was somehow a more crucial and promising link in the whole affair than anything else.

Later, seated at the old desk in his study, a pot of coffee before him and Nelson about somewhere else in the flat, he sought to remember anything odd or out of the way in the narrative of Peter Graham the previous day. He and Pierce had gone over that again on the way back from the prison and there was only one thing which stood out in any way in Cheyney's mind. It was an apparently complete absence of girls in young Tommy's life. Of course, his father could not speak for his son's life at Cambridge – and was vigorously opposed to the idea that Tommy was in any way homosexual – but, pressed by Pierce, he stressed rather than undercut the idea that Tommy was not interested in girls, certainly not those of his own age.

That last thought formulated, Cheyney wondered what it was that had made him think it. He lit a pipe and walked furiously up and down in the limited space between the front of his desk and the large and unnamed household plant which stood in the window recess. A scrap of dialogue came back to him. Pierce had said: 'Do you mean the boy wasn't interested in women at all?' 'Not live ones.' Graham stopped, and almost gave a half-smile. 'I mean, he went to films and things, and watched television. But it was always the older actresses he seemed to like.'

And that, Cheyney thought, was hardly a very seminal piece of information. Today, Pierce's men would be combing through Tommy's associates and connections, especially at Cambridge, but wherever else he went as well. The parental home would come apart under their ministrations, and even Maria Graham would be subjected to Pierce's inexhaustible questioning. There was certainly little Cheyney could do in competition with them. If there was, perhaps, an older woman somewhere in Tommy's life, she would be found; of that he was morally certain.

Still, somehow, Cheyney felt that amid the meagre material before him there was something he should and could latch on to. He had never been a good team man, and he groaned both at the thought of all the work the police were now doing with which he could not compete, and the backbreaking task of sifting through it which would later face him for, bad team man or no, his temperament would not allow him to leave it to Pierce to present him with a synopsis of what he had uncovered.

At nine Cheyney rang Miss Levison to say that he would not be coming into the office, thereby unloading on her yet another collection of problems. He switched his telephone through to her office and left it to her to decide who he should talk to. Then, in his study, the only room where he allowed his mask of restraint and coldness to slip, he smoked and brooded and walked and scribbled on bits of paper.

Midday found him gazing in abstracted fashion into the long tank of tropical fish which topped a bookcase in one corner of his room. He could not expect to hear from Pierce before the end of the day; he would not ring the Yard however frustrated he felt; and his musings had got him precisely nowhere. Nelson had gone, taking Bruce with him as usual for the second tramp of the day, and Cheyney felt he could bear it no longer.

Though he was before all else a Scot and a countryman, Cheyney found great pleasure in London; and though he could not wholly subscribe to Dr Johnson's dictum, because he loved his native Galloway so much, it was often in long and solitary strolls through the grubby streets of the capital that he reckoned to pacify his mind, and sometimes even to resolve problems that had been irking him. He looked out of the window and saw that, though the weather was still cold and threatening, the rain had, for the moment, stopped. He made up his mind, put on a suit of old tweeds, and set out for a walk, planning to ramble about until hunger struck him, and trusting then to find some tolerable bistro in which to eat.

He had walked for half an hour and, as he was going down the Strand, he had the sudden conviction that he was being followed. A conviction of that kind, to a man like Cheyney, with his experience of life and action in strange places, was as palpable a piece of evidence as though he had seen a black-cloaked stranger ducking into an alleyway as he looked over his shoulder. He had, however, never been followed in London before; and it gave him a strange and prickly feeling. It gave him also, nonetheless, an upsurge of confidence, for at that stage in his walk he had reached the very depths of intellectual depression, and had half-convinced himself that he and Pierce had been chasing moon-beams for six months: he had even got to the stage of devising explanations for the black plastic badges which would dispose of any association between Tommy Graham and the earlier incidences of discovery.

The hairs on the back of his neck stiffened slightly even on this chilly day. He stopped to buy cigarettes, and idled at a news-stand, every sense and every instinct turned outwards, turned towards the passing, peeling, scurrying crowd of people in the Strand, who always seemed to be shopping, but never stopped save to window-shop. Somewhere among them was the somebody whose presence Cheyney had recognised at some point during his stroll. Cheyney bumped into another man and met with a curse: he was trying to remember at what point his mind had detected another presence. Certainly, it seemed later than the departure from his flat. But when he left the flat he had been so deeply frustrated and disappointed with his complete failure to arrive at any solution to the major problem that confronted him that his instincts might not have been in very good shape. Also, he was a man disposed to take particular delight in small pleasures, and he remembered that he had been irritated by the fact that, when he had decided to make one of his long London tramps, Bruce was not available, because with Nelson. So, he had to think when his mind had begun to function properly, begun to be aware of a hostile presence in a way it could never be when he was sitting in his official car, or leaning back in his office chair. Cheyney realised again: he had never been followed in London before; but his life in London was one – what with cars and servants and secretaries to protect him – which virtually precluded an effective tail.

So, for the first time in eight years, Colonel Cheyney felt lost. Of course he could turn into any telephone box, and make sure that his own highly efficient and silent people – or Pierce's less committed, but nonetheless capable, servants – picked him up and found the follower, but that would frustrate the one tangible discovery he had made in the last six months. For being tailed was a proof that he and Pierce had not merely been beating at the air, like a pair of kittens.

It was – he had now worked it out – exactly eight and a half years since Cheyney had been confronted with the problem of what an expert should do with a follower – assuming that he was not now cracking up, and that there really was somebody watching his progress down the tatty and overblown Strand. One could elude pursuit: but that presumed that there was nothing to learn from the tail. One could turn and kill: but that was necessary only if one's business was exceptionally pressing, or if some purpose could be served by killing, or if the tail meant to kill one. Was this tail out for Cheyney's life – in the Strand? One could detect the tail and confront him. One could follow the tail – that was the most sophisticated problem and solution of all; but Cheyney, with an appreciation of his own deficiencies with which few colleagues would have credited him, realised he was no longer good enough for that.

Nothing, then nothing, except the conviction that there was a follower. For a couple of hundred yards Cheyney fell victim to the self-doubt of all professionals. He stopped to buy more cigarettes, not because he needed them, but because he was trying to detect the follower he knew was there. Then he cursed himself, because he thought that this second purchase would convince the tail that he had been detected. Then he thought again: if the man was following Colonel Cheyney he would have expected – if properly briefed – a variance of behaviour patterns, because Cheyney was the kind of figure, legendary in the profession, who would be expected always to be on his guard. It would require an amazing mind to notice that, on his London strolls, or in Galloway, Cheyney was not a spy at all, but a gentleman. He wished he had his dog with him. Eight and a half years ago Cheyney had, in Istanbul, turned and killed a tail; and it had required all his skill to extricate himself from the consequences.

But – if the conviction that told him he was being followed was right – hard though it was to believe in London – Cheyney was on the verge of a great discovery. Unless an old enemy had arisen to haunt him, there could be nothing to justify tailing Colonel Cheyney except his work of months' standing on the black plastic badges. But Cheyney needed thinking time. As he reached the mouth of Chancery Lane, he turned into the Old Cock for a pint and a sandwich. He took a booth at the back, and waited to see what – apart from the riff-raff of law students – followed him in. He had a little time – a very little time – to think. Unfortunately, three men, as middle-aged as himself, came in, along with the law students: none looked like a tail. But he was then so out of tune with the business that he could hardly tell.

For the moment, however, Cheyney had a refuge. He could perfectly safely, and without arousing any doubts, stay in the pub for some time yet; or at least as long as his follower was convinced that his long walk was exactly what it was – aimless. He might even, he speculated, make a telephone call – but he quickly rejected that course as too risky. He thought he had better stoke up for what was clearly going to be an uncertain afternoon, and perhaps even an uncertain evening. He went to the bar and acquired another sandwich and a large whisky – who knew what demands might yet be made on his bladder? He then returned to his table to address himself to the central question – what party in the complex thing he was investigating would want to have him followed?

Like most people in Britain who do highly secret work Cheyney's life was an open book. Nelson provided some protection for him at his London home, but his house in Scotland was quite unguarded. He was in the telephone directory, in *Who's Who* and in half a dozen other directories of important, or at least established, people. No rival secret service would have the slightest difficulty in assassinating him: such things rarely happened unless one was quite out of one's base, if only because assassination was a game that could be played both ways, and no national espionage or counter-espionage organisation wanted to start a private war.

Of course, Cheyney reminded himself, since the widespread rise of terror – Irish terror, Arab terror (Cheyney cared for neither race) – almost anything could happen, especially to a man whose reputation was well known in most of the shadier corners of the world, where men gathered to plot revolution, destruction and change. But a moment's reflection convinced Cheyney that none of these enemies of principle would set a tail on him – even supposed that they had among their number a man skilled enough to avoid Cheyney's own counter-scrutiny. Their method would be, as usual, the unanswerable sneak attack, the knife in the back, the bullet in the dark, or the bomb that would kill so many it was likely that their target would be among the dead. After twenty-five more minutes Cheyney finished his drink and left the tavern.

The sky had darkened again while he had been inside and the clouds now leered down over that winding channel which is Fleet Street. It would not, Cheyney thought, turn to rain just yet, but it was going to be an increasingly heavy, oppressive, threatening afternoon. Cheyney, who loved bad weather in the country, hated it in the city, and he shuddered, metaphorically turning up his collar. Now he began

36

to walk more briskly, down towards Ludgate Circus, hurrying against the flow of indifferent, racing humanity. His mind was made up now, and he no longer sought to spy out the man – or men – behind him. He stopped, as though irresolute, at the foot of Fleet Street, and bought an *Evening Standard*. He waited to cross the road beside a young and immensely serious looking policeman and wondered how the man would react if Cheyney were to approach him, show him the small card which every policeman is taught to recognise, and ask for help. It would be a silly thing to do, of course, but Cheyney grinned at the thought of the reaction he would get. Would the bobby draw a whistle? Did they still carry whistles, by the way? Then, his moment of humour suddenly past, he felt bleak and lonely and oppressed, not just because he was threatened in the press of London – which seemed absurd – but because he was threatened in an area of London which, above all, was one in which his situation would command interest, activity, energy.

Cheyney moved down Farringdon Street towards Farringdon bridge. He noted, with that pleasurable quickening of the instincts that always came to him in this particular part of London, the almost abrupt change between the increasingly featureless and tatty commercialism which he was leaving behind, and the equally tatty, but somehow much more alive semi-slums which he was entering. Hart's the butcher's, for example, on Hart's Corner, and the elongated roadside bookstall – there would be no room for them back in the Strand or in Fleet Street itself, for they would not command attention, nor would they have survived the heavier traffic and the narrower streets of the urban swell behind him.

He was already in much less populated territory. He stopped at the bookstall, and gave his attention for some ten minutes to its wares. He was resolutely not trying to pick up the tracker, but he felt the skin on the back of his neck crawl anyway, and he knew that the enemy was still there. Another man came up beside him, one improbably attired in the most ancient of tweed overcoats, a scarf of incredible length wrapped again and again around his neck and still having sufficient length to reach his knees, topped by the darkest of glasses and the most battered of cloth caps. This individual was wearing woollen gloves with the fingers cut off and his nails and hands were grimy beyond belief. Muttering away to himself he began to sort through the books under the increasingly careful eye of the stall keeper. Cheyney, the bookseller paid no attention to: his tweeds were old, and far from well pressed, but his bearing was of the kind that protected him from suspicion and scrutiny.

Except the scrutiny of whatever was behind him. Except that. His mind now made up, Cheyney felt that brief but gratifying prickliness of the skin which always came to him at moments like this. He bought an ancient Palgrave and crossed the road again, heading for Mace Alley.

Crossing the road gave him, of course, a perfectly legitimate opportunity to glance about him. Here there was no press of people, but there was sufficient number to make it impossible for him, in a quick look, to pick out whoever had made him a target. Yet he was more convinced than ever that somebody was *there*. Somebody was at his back. Still, he had drawn the enemy away from an area of high human density into one much more sparsely occupied. Only one move remained.

Idling at the bookstall had given Cheyney the opportunity to slow down the whole operation. Now he speeded up, walking quickly – far more quickly than he had walked down Fleet Street – up the left hand side of Farringdon Street and towards the anonymous confusion of buildings, occupied and derelict, which lay away to his left. He turned down one mean street and then another, not pausing, not waiting, not looking.

And then he was in Mace Alley. To his right was a terrace of houses and shops, a few still functioning, the rest abandoned, shuttered, ghosts. To his left as he hurried along the narrow pathway was a site from which the buildings had already been razed, the fence that excluded his sight from what lay beyond it made of corrugated iron. This was territory Cheyney knew, and when he went again to the left he quickly found the loose panel which it took him but a second to swing back, and only another to get behind.

And then he waited, no longer the tweedy city stroller, pub luncher, book buyer. The same sort of change came over him as Graham had seen in Pierce's office the day before. His skin tautened and his eyes began to burn. All his attention, all his energy, was now directed outwards: he could not have made a mistake.

It was only seconds before he heard the hesitant footsteps. The two sides of the narrow little alley had a slight echo creating effect, and he could hear from some distance. The tracker was obviously in a quandary, for he had entered empty country, and he could not be sure that it was safe to follow along. Cheyney heard him first rush on – a quick patter of feet – and then stop as he came to the corner. It was the most difficult of situations, for the craft required in a place like this was more that of the country than that of the city, and if the unknown enemy was a city spy, however well equipped mentally and with experience, he would be in danger of psychic loss. But it was his alteration of pace that convinced Cheyney he had his man, and could not now go wrong.

Cheyney chose his moment carefully and expertly. One second the man had arrived at the loose panel, the next the panel had been flung back and Cheyney had drawn him with one powerful hand into the waste land behind. The fingers of Cheyney's left hand took the man by the throat and the long and powerful arm hauled. As the body passed, Cheyney's right hand swung in a brief chopping movement and then the mysterious tracker was lying unconscious beneath him.

No, Cheyney realised, he had not spotted the man at all; he had no memory of that face in any of his backward glances. It was a medium face, slightly tight, slightly mean. It was the face of a man of perhaps forty, nondescript but carefully and neatly, if cheaply dressed. He was wearing . . .

And as he reached this point Cheyney realised the mistake he had made.

'That was neat, Colonel Cheyney,' said the calm voice behind him, 'but you must be a little past this kind of thing. No – please don't move or turn around.'

There was the light but unmistakable touch of a gun in Cheyney's back and it was then instantly withdrawn. Bitterness flowed over Cheyney: he had attended to his instinct in the fundamental thing – that he was being followed – but not enough, for he had scarcely listened to the voice that had told him there might be more than one of them. He had been beautifully, comprehensively, taken.

CHAPTER FIVE

Captivity

Bitter self-disgust returned to Cheyney at the same time as consciousness. It was typical of him that, as soon as he awoke, he recalled the quiet voice and the gun in his back, and realised that, although his attacker might have been ambidexterous, it was likely that he had had a job to transfer the gun from his right to his left hand before he had sandbagged Cheyney. There had thus been a moment – a moment, no more than that – when Cheyney could have turned on him, and he had failed to seize it.

The self-disgust was due to Cheyney's awareness of his failure to dominate. Clarity of thought comes as often with pain as through alcohol. In that minute or two in which Cheyney came awake in an adequately sized but inadequately furnished bedroom he saw himself both as colleagues and subordinates and inadequates and Miss Levison saw him; and as he thought he ought to be judged. They thought him peerless: his reputation was superb; nobody among the enemy had ever opposed him and survived; no colleague had ever gone against him and won. He was immensely fit, immensely skilled, immensely his own man. To himself, as he looked at cretonne curtains and saw the bars on the windows beyond, Cheyney was a middle-aged man who had been made a fool of, and in that very area of activity which he had made his own, and on his achievement in which the respect, the regard and the fear of others was founded.

For another five minutes Cheyney was a wounded animal. He found himself lying on a garish duvet. Almost unconscious, he inspected his prison, and found it secure. The barred window, the steel-sheeted door, the absence in the room of anything that might be made into a weapon – even the light came from a wall panel fronted by un-breakable glass, so a bulb could not be taken and used as a stabbing weapon – demonstrated how professional were his captors, and how great his own folly. He staggered to a mirror – made of plastic; its shards would not be weapons – and saw the dreadful amount of blood in his eyes, produced, no doubt, by concussion. He looked in his pockets: his cigarette case had gone; but his cigarettes, he saw, were on the table beside the bed. He tested – the table was irremovably bolted to the floor. His lighter had gone. And there was no box of matches – they could be made into a weapon – but a book beside the meticulously un-loaded cigarettes on the table. Ashtray? There was a plastic wastepaper basket. When he saw that Cheyney realised he had been padding around in stockinged feet: his shoes, too, had been taken away.

The wounded animal returned to the bed and lit a cigar-ette. Because it was Cheyney it began to piece together bits of information. This prison was secure, but not luxurious, nor well-appointed. It was not, Cheyney's in-stinct told him, the citadel of the enemy he and Pierce had been chasing. *They* would have been either cruder – a cellar, perhaps – or more luxurious. Cheyney closed his eyes and began to will his headache to go away. He almost slept with the cigarette between the fingers of his right hand. He almost slept – but not quite. He was trying to relax himself – everything about him – in order to destroy both the pain in his head and the self-disgust. He was trying to make himself himself again: he was trying to return from being a wounded animal to being Colonel Cheyney. He put his thoughts into almost those words and almost grinned. That was the first stage to recovery.

However hard and tough and trained a man may be in Cheyney's profession, if he does not regularly see and experience action he weakens, however carefully and systematically he uses his skill and reputation to impose his fame on those who work closely to him. If he sees too much action he dies, not necessarily by an enemy's hand, but by the dissolution of himself made by pressure – wounds and strain – of events. Until now, Cheyney told himself, he had had it easy. His career had been brilliant – embarrassments and enemies alike had been swept out of the way. Because he both believed so strongly in his personal ideology of patriotism as to be able to ignore the compromises and inadequacies of the politicians he served, and because he had been so supremely successful in his own skills, he had become feared by friends and enemies alike, but also invaluable. Now, for the first time in ten years, he was in the unknown.

Cheyney let himself drift away. The cigarette dipped, every muscle became relaxed, he deliberately reduced his anger, his annoyance and his hate, because he had to kill the pain in his head, had to recover his self-esteem, had to re-establish his authority. He began to forget the room, began to remember his great days – Quemoy, Korea, being in Yugoslavia at the behest of Philby and realising that his whole team was doomed – and then getting out of it. Suddenly he found that reminiscence – even reminiscence of oneself – is a strength. There was no more he could do, no anger about his folly in Mace Alley, no way of escape from this room, until he was summoned.

How long he spent in this mood he could not afterwards remember. He awoke to a voice, and felt an absurd pleasure in the fact that the man who owned that voice was genuinely astonished to find Cheyney genuinely asleep.

The message of the voice, however, put the whole day in its place.

'Get up. Mr Grey wants to see you.'

'Get me my shoes.'

The man – a brute, large, pock-marked and carrying a Luger – seemed to expect the instruction and nodded out into the corridor. A much smaller creature came in and Cheyney spent a few moments putting on his shoes. There were a few moments of furious thought. He had been taken by Clement Grey – who clearly still carried a good deal of clout – and not the mysterious enemy he and Pierce had been pursuing. That, suddenly, explained the physical character of his prison. The mixed elaboration and inadequacy of its décor was typical of the British underworld: it lacked the style either of brutal simplicity or luxury. But it was efficient, and in this too it was typical. So, Cheyney realised, the absconding Grey had taken the offensive.

Once outside his room Cheyney could get a sense of the size of the house, and even of its location. The cramped corridor, giving an illusion of length, made it, in his judgment, what used to be called a villa, and probably one in the Home Counties. It had been decorated – once – in greens and yellows, but the decoration had not been made to last. It had once been the property of somebody who would do it over once every couple of years. But the light provided by naked bulbs in wall brackets revealed that nothing had been done for a very long time. The place had not that solidity of structure that could retain even an unkempt dignity in spite of carelessness: it was grimy, musty and flyblown. A huge dead cheese plant stood sentry at the top of the surprisingly generous stairs down which they turned, to face an adequate hall, inadequately lit by a chandelier made for a dozen bulbs, now containing four, unsheathed. Cheyney felt a touch of desolation, not at his own condition, but at a house – any house – abused.

44

The smaller creature – as Cheyney thought of him – furtive and bent and smelling of stale sweat, darted ahead of them to open the right-hand door. His elephantine companion came right up behind Cheyney and a hand flat on one shoulder blade sent him staggering, unbalanced, into the room. He recovered and turned, which brought him, halfway round, to his second major shock of the day.

In a heavy, straight armchair sat Superintendent Pierce.

His arms were strapped tightly and cruelly to the knobbled wooden arms of the chair. His head lay drunkenly back against it, and blood seeped slowly from one corner of a bruised and disfigured mouth. His shirt and jacket were wet, and an empty bucket stood just in front of him. He had clearly only just been brought round. It took his glazed eyes a moment to focus, but even though they noted Cheyney the discipline of a lifetime forbade even a badly hurt Pierce to acknowledge surprise, shock or relief. Battered and crushed, he was still imperturbable.

'He hasn't spoken a word,' said a grating voice behind Cheyney.

The last time Cheyney had seen Clement Grey the man had been in the dock. They had never spoken, because Cheyney had preferred to leave the examination of Grey, both before and after his trial, to Pierce. He had recognised a character beyond his own range, though it should have been well within the range of Pierce. Now he began to wonder: the house, its trappings, the thugs who had brought him down – all these were standard practice since the Krays and the Richardsons had begun improving on the heritage left them by Billy Hill and Jack Como. But the actions Grey had already taken, the kidnapping of Superintendent Pierce and of Colonel Cheyney, were in a different imaginative range, a crazy range, perhaps, suggesting that Grey was not just a not wholly sane man who

45

loved killing, but a brute of perversion beyond the dreams, even now, of British gangsters.

Grey allowed Cheyney to inspect him for a long moment. He was a big man, but not remarkably so, standing perhaps just under six feet, and sitting now behind a long table desk of Edwardian design and some shabbiness. He had a gaunt face with hugely hollowed cheeks, topped by a mop of black hair kept in order only by regular and rigorous trimming. It was coarse in texture as were his hands, locked together in macabre similarity to those of Pierce when he was behind his own desk, covered with identically coarse hair, long and simian in their power and inhumanity. His eye-sockets, like his cheeks, were small caverns, flat and deep, brown, gleaming, suggestive of animal vitality, and dominant. It was in them that, in his brief moment of inspection, Cheyney sought for some understanding of this wholly unexpected opponent, for they were not the eyes of a thug, however manic, however self-willed.

There was something oddly desperate in Grey's make-up, and Cheyney recalled that he had sensed it in court. On the surface the man was the standard imitative gangster, first modelled in America during prohibition and developed into a literary artefact by Dashiell Hammett and Raymond Chandler. He had most of the vices of the British version of the model – a pseudo-American twang in his voice, though it was as much suppressed as emphasised, a cultivation of menace, a hint too much swagger in the walk and too much flash in the clothes. But there was added to an evidently total amorality something else, a strange poetry of anarchic but managed violence. Grey reeked of a barely restrained, barely controlled *amour* with violence, the more threatening because wholly and completely unintellectualised. Now he nodded – again, it was a weird parody of those moments when Pierce deigned to

46

notice another member of the human race by moving his head – and gestured with his left hand.

An unresisting Cheyney was taken and, neither roughly nor gently, installed in another chair next to Pierce. To his surprise – for with all his concentration on Grey he was furiously registering things around him as well – he was not bound. Deliberately moving his head he turned again to look at his colleague. There was no doubt that he had been systematically and cruelly beaten, but without sophistication or perversion. He was badly knocked about, and such a beating as he had received – probably for the first time – could be terribly damaging to a man in middle age. He was now very helpless, and very deeply humiliated. What had happened to him was outside the range of experience normal for a senior policeman, and well beyond the call of duty for such: it was with real and unfeigned horror that Cheyney saw the dark and extra dampness round his crotch. Pierce was not, then, wholly immune to the weaknesses of his fellow-men in the face of violence and sadism. Cheyney was shocked, not because such beatings were outside *his* experience but because the violence and humiliation involved were necessarily outside the experience of Pierce. Yet, even while he pitied, a touch of irritation entered his regard when he met Pierce's eyes. They were the same as ever, unmoved, unmoving, pitiless, watching.

'I know coppers,' said Grey in his flat, gunmetal voice. 'They're not supposed to be able to take it. They're not like your lot, Colonel Cheyney.' There was a hint of sarcastic emphasis in his use of the title. 'But there's not been a peep out of him, Colonel. Not a peep. Maybe I've got it wrong and he's tougher than you are.'

Cheyney looked across the room at him. Another man, he saw, had joined them and come up on the right. A young tearaway, big, muscular, shirt open to the waist and a

47

medallion of some sort around his neck. Eyes open, vacant, a weapon in his right hand. Menace, a corrupt, brooding, hateful menace filled the shabby, untutored room. Cheyney was relaxed – he even slouched slightly in his chair to get more comfortable – and though unarmed and helpless for a moment he held the whole room. 'For this,' he said, 'I will kill you.'

The new arrival snickered, but Grey took the statement seriously enough. He shook his head. 'Not yet you won't, and in a little while I won't care whether you do or not.' He wrung his long powerful fingers together until the knuckles shone. 'I want the answer to only one question. I don't want to beat up coppers, and I certainly wouldn't have wanted to tangle with you and your lot. But read this well – I know that I'm all washed up, and I want that answer before I go. Y'see I'm going to do something, and after that I'll take my chances. I want you and this fool here to understand that. When you've helped me you'll go free. The longer you take to help me the more I'll hurt you. I'll break your bodies into little pieces. You'll still want to go free, but after a few days it may not be worth it. But understand me – I don't care. Whatever is left of you will be free. You have my word on that and you'll learn to trust my word. You'll learn to trust my word when I say that this operation is my swansong. Do you think I'm a fool?' – his voice rose several angry notches – 'I know I can't get away with bashing you and Pierce. Your boys or his will get me, because it will get out that it *was* me. But while you're here you will also learn to trust the other thing I say, that you will go free when you answer my question. I wanted you to see Pierce because you're not as hidebound as he is. You don't care so much about the bloody rules. You may have the sense to see that I mean what I say, and to see that you can get me when it's over, if you can find me. You may have the sense to see that I'll break both of you in bits unless I get what I want, and that it's in your interest to give it me.'

The balance of psychological advantage, only momentarily with Cheyney, had shifted. With genuine academic interest Cheyney said:

'You say you'll free us. But we'll be after the goons as well. What about them?'

He almost expected the answer, but could not believe it until it was said. Grey smiled, an open, cheerful smile in a closed face. 'Hit him, Charlie,' he said. 'Not hard, but hit him.'

The newcomer stepped round in front of Cheyney and swung his right hand. A barber's stropping leather swished through the air and slashed across Cheyney's face. His brain felt as though it had been lifted out and pummelled. He was too agonised, too numbed, even to respond as the excruciating pain swept through his head. All he could see through his pain was the powerful, muscular body of the animal that had struck and the grinning face superimposed on the slightly drooling mouth. The blow killed his reflexes and he slumped back in the chair. Then the face was gone and Grey was talking again.

The twang had gone from his voice: he spoke almost as an educated man. 'The things I use, Cheyney, the things I use this time, don't understand consequence. That right, Albert?'

Cheyney dragged his pain-racked face around to the big man who had brought him down. The horrendous, pock-marked face split into an uneasy grin. 'Sure, boss.' He looked at Cheyney and licked his cream slice lips.

'Right, Simmy?'

On a neck that was suddenly a very insubstantial stalk indeed for his burning head Cheyney looked round the other way, almost unable to see, now, the bony little face of the third man.

'Oh sure, boss.'

'There are four more in this house like that, Cheyney.'

Grey, Cheyney knew in his pain, was totally in charge and utterly right. His was an animal power, the power of a pack leader: his followers could not think nor reason even about their own interest. He held them completely in the spell of his power. But he himself was rational; and he understood perfectly well that the underworld would learn how Clement Grey had used his men, and that Cheyney's and Pierce's departments would have the help of the underworld in disposing of him. He knew that, and he told Cheyney how well he knew it. That was a measure not only of his power, but of the strength of his word. What he was conveying to Cheyney as he had failed to convey to Pierce was that he was above any considerations, prudential, Machiavellian, or personal, in the single-minded pursuit of whatever aim he had in mind. In the odd light of the room that caged and disciplined beast, utterly without capacity for remorse or terror, was life to his own men: that was why they would follow him unquestioningly, for they did not grasp the higher capacity he had for articulating a purpose and evaluating a sacrifice. Leader of the pack he was as he sat there with his powerful fingers strangling one another and his deep eyes burning, but he was an animal, only one stage further on in evolution.

'What,' said Cheyney calmly, but with a dreadful fear that he already knew, 'do you want?'

'I want a man and a woman. But above all, and from you, I want the answer to a question.'

Then, as Cheyney somehow already knew he would, he picked up one of the plastic badges and held it with the Q facing Cheyney.

'You have had six months, and with your resources you must know something by now. Where is Mr Quex?'

CHAPTER SIX

Pierce Takes a Hand

Had his position not been so desperate and his pain so great
– bolts of agony were shooting into his head from the weal
across his face – Cheyney might have laughed. Here in
this grim and unknown room, facing a gangster both intelligent and barbarous, he and Pierce at the same time
had had their first real breakthrough. It was perfectly true
that the name Quex meant nothing whatever to him, but
it explained the emblazoned Q, and he did not doubt that
Grey had insisted on knowing who he worked for before
undertaking the drastic rescue of Oldfield. It seemed impossible that, if he could only get away, he could not, with
all his and Pierce's resources, find Quex, and find out what
he was.

He tightened his grip on the arms of his chair and considered before he replied to the question, looking steadily
all the time into the unnaturally large and unnaturally
brown eyes of one of the most desperate creatures he had
ever faced. He had to steady his voice before he could
speak.

'What has Pierce told you? Be frank with me, please.'

'Don't come parade-ground with me,' Grey snarled, and
for a moment he almost lost his control, revealing for an
instant that, beneath the iron grip his will and brain imposed on his emotions, he was still the street corner thug
who had clawed his way to power in his own brutal world
through the terror he could impose. Then:

'I told you. He said not one bloody word.'

51

'He had nothing to say.' Cheyney leant forward very slightly and Charlie moved with him. 'We know nothing. We know there is something going on, and we know that it's big. We know you were involved. And we've seen' – he gestured – 'those badges. But we knew nothing of anybody called Quex until this minute, and certainly nothing of any woman. Who is she, by the way?'

Grey rose from behind the table and again filled the room with his *manic* force. For a few seconds Cheyney had felt he could reason with Grey; now, in a chill instant, he doubted it.

Grey walked round the table with a springing step and stood over Cheyney. He took Cheyney's face in a long, hairy paw, and stared down at him. The burning in his eyes was now really insane, and Cheyney was frightened. Grey held him that way, while Cheyney strove to relax, for what seemed like an hour.

'You will learn,' said Grey, and it was clear he was making a titanic effort not to smash everything in sight, including his two prisoners. 'You will learn not to lie to me. The police and the Secret Service and God knows how many other lots have been working on this for six months. I know that. I know that you want to break up a ring. I told you – no ring matters a bugger to me. I want a man and a woman. I want Quex. I haven't much time. Give him to me and I'll do your job for you. I'll cut the balls out from between his fat legs and I'll make him choke on them. And if you get Quex you'll break your ring. Just give him to me.'

He let Cheyney's head go and walked back behind his table. Suddenly, he said:

'Are you interested in history, Mr Cheyney?'

'Somewhat.'

Grey softened, almost smiled. In a sort of ghastly crooning voice he said, 'In the Peninsular War against Napoleon there was a Spaniard, a terrorist I guess you'd call him, who had something against a French general. He said if he got him he'd cut him into slices, starting with the feet. He did. I might do that to Quex, Mr Cheyney.'

Charlie said: 'Gee, boss,' and licked his lips for the sheer delight of the spectacle.

Cheyney said, again evenly: 'For sending you over?' He had sensed a relaxation in Grey, and sought to prolong the moment and, if he could, gain from it.

'That, and other things.' In a second Grey had lost control again. He swung his hand and knocked a bottle and glass off the table to smash on the floor. 'And you and you,' he screamed at Cheyney and Pierce. 'You, you bastards, you know something and I want it now.'

His face was suddenly mottled and contorted and thrombotic and then the rage had gone again. He sat there, hands twisting into one another, head bent, eyes fixed on them, fighting for control of himself. Cheyney looked on him, not without pity, until Simmy appeared from behind him, carrying another bottle and glass. Grey poured himself a huge whisky – three-quarters at least of a tumbler – and swallowed. Cheyney, in his gentlest voice, asked the grand question.

'Who is the woman, Grey?'

For a moment he thought he had made a mistake that would literally be fatal. Then Grey smiled that open smile again, and said, pointing to Pierce:

'Ask him. He'll know.'

Not, Cheyney thought as he turned to look at Pierce, 'He knows,' but 'He'll know,' meaning, 'He'll be able to guess.' But Pierce, if he was capable of guessing aloud, was not going to do it now. He turned his disfigured face away from Cheyney and looked stonily at the other wall. Cheyney waited, but Pierce was not going to speak, and Grey did not. He tried another tack.

53

'Grey,' he said, 'I know you don't believe me now, but I have told you the truth. When you took Oldfield we guessed you were part of the big operation we believed existed. But I swear to you, man, I have learned more tonight than I have in the last six months. Whatever you know it is more than I have.'

'Are you offering me a deal?' The question was snapped out.

Cheyney shook his head.

'Well, I'll offer you a deal, Colonel Cheyney. I'll offer you the same deal as I offered you when you came in here. I don't believe you, Cheyney. *I don't believe you*, and I'll have taken you and this other bugger apart before I think of changing my mind. To me, Cheyney, you and this poor bugger here are just a short cut. Just a short cut, that's all. I may have to go around a bit longer. That won't bother me much, and you'll suffer for it.'

'Grey,' said Cheyney, starting again.

'Shut up. You have till first light tomorrow to remember what I want to know, after that Simmy and Jacko get you, and your friends can have the rest. Shackle him.'

Something went with a little click in Cheyney's head: it was the snapping of the self-control he had shown so far, the cracking of the diplomatic mask assumed to beguile a man intelligent and powerful, but not really sane.

'So that's all you are,' he said in a voice like ice, 'just a thug, just a roustabout. You can't even think.'

But Grey had lost interest and what might, again, have been fatal, passed almost without notice. Then Albert's gun was in Cheyney's back again and Charlie had clicked Cheyney's wrists into handcuffs.

'Take them up, you two,' said Grey. 'Let them talk, and get to work on them at dawn. I don't want to see them again until first light.'

54

The gusts having swept him, his indifference was plain and unfeigned.

Charlie, too, now had a gun in the hand from the wrist of which dangled, by a loop, his barber's stropping leather. He swung Cheyney round by his left shoulder, always keeping the gun carefully and expertly out of reach and conveying, in his wonderfully supple movement, and through his lax grin, the jolliest hope that his captive would try to take it away. A deep despair swept over Cheyney.

Albert, meanwhile, had unstrapped Pierce from the chair. He pulled the policeman roughly to his feet: Pierce's head lolled and blood began to come freshly from his mouth. Albert slapped him roughly, and Cheyney started involuntarily forward, to be swung out of his direction with a punch in the back from Charlie and sent sprawling. As he got uncomfortably to his feet, he saw that Albert was keeping Pierce on his feet by twisting the man's left arm halfway up his back and relying on the pain thus created to force into Pierce the will to make his legs work again. As they moved unsteadily out into the hallway and began the intolerable journey up the stairs Pierce uttered his first sound. It was a wretched groan and, though Cheyney could not see his face, he could imagine the terrible contortions imposed on it as the sudden and greater pain of being suspended by the socket of his left arm caused his will to call for consciousness and force the other extremities of his body to give that wretched member some support.

Halfway up the stairs, and in spite of Albert's brutal strength, Pierce began to fall forward. Albert instantly let go, as though remembering Grey's order that the rough stuff was to wait until dawn, and stood warily down a step. Charlie's hand halted Cheyney, and he too retreated. They stood there, almost in single file for a moment before Albert swung his boot, not too heavily, at Pierce's backside. The wretched man groaned again and Albert said, 'C'mon, get yourself up,' but in a voice suddenly gruff, and not unkind.

He reached out for Pierce's collar and lifted, rather than hauled, his victim to his feet, so smoothly and powerfully that, for a few seconds, Pierce's scrabbling feet dangled in mid-air. Then they were on the move again, Pierce propelled relentlessly upwards by main force of Albert's left arm, Cheyney, his hands manacled in front of him – strange, was his fleeting thought, how that destroys one's balance – prodded by Charlie's hand and gun. At last they were at the top. Pierce stumbled forward again as Albert let go of his collar, whipped huge fingers round his upper arm, steadied him thus, and took his fearful wristhold again. What, Cheyney wondered, had they done to Pierce, and what was in store?

They were only a few feet from the door when Pierce stumbled again. Albert paused and Charlie cursed, as he and Cheyney came up on the left. Then it happened. Albert must have loosened his grip on a victim he thought wholly helpless. With an invisible twist Pierce had freed his wrist, swung, taken Albert's right arm, knocked the gun out of his hand, and swung his huge bulk against Cheyney, who cannoned into Charlie as Charlie cannoned against the wall.

A moment later Albert was dead. Pierce had never lost hold of his right wrist and continued the swing. Suddenly, he halted it and, legs planted wide apart, stopped Albert again in his tracks, using his free arm to apply terrible traction to the relationship between arm and body. Before Albert's scream had become more than a gurgle, Pierce's ringed fist had smashed his teeth back into his throat and, as he released an already unconscious man to fall, the heel of his left hand came over and broke his neck.

Nor was Cheyney in any worse situation. Off balance he had found Charlie's stomach with his elbow and, in the next flowing movement, rocked back on the balance of his left foot to take the gun before it could be fired. Physically, Charlie was a much less formidable proposition than Albert, and he was already winded. Steadying himself, Cheyney kicked the man in the stomach and bent him double. As Charlie's head came over towards his own stomach, he took it lovingly to him, brought one of his manacled hands up on either side of it, crossed his hands at the back of the head and heaved. A moment later he dropped Charlie, to stare with sightless and bulging eyes, and to point with protruding tongue, at a blank wall, the decoration on which was fraying.

Gasping, Cheyney turned to face Pierce.

It had to have been a supreme effort. The Superintendent had managed to pick up Albert's gun, but he was now leaning back against the wall, and it was dangling by the trigger guard from his fingers. His left hand supported himself by the buttocks and his breath was rasping through his open and bloody mouth. He could scarcely speak, and his face was purple with pain and exertion. Cheyney nodded quickly in salutation and turned to the bodies.

Thirty seconds later he was free, having found the keys to his cuffs, not to mention his treasured cigarette case, in Charlie's pockets. The odds, he computed, were now six to four, and he and Pierce had surprise weapons, for he doubted if their scuffle had made enough noise to attract the household.

Back, then, to Pierce. Pierce had made another great effort, and was now almost upright. He managed a woefully lopsided grin, the first Cheyney had ever seen on his face, and allowed himself a second of triumph. 'Middle-aged coppers,' he said. 'Well...' and then he fainted.

CHAPTER SEVEN

The Woman in the Case

Cheyney crouched on one knee by Pierce. Even their desperate situation could not kill his admiration for that taciturn creature. Pierce's collapse, after disposing of Albert in as clinical and final a manner as Cheyney himself could have managed at peak form, made it clear that he had not been shamming, had not made pretence to a hurt greater than had been inflicted on him. But Cheyney, the conscious one, knew how bad things were. Had he and Pierce both been reasonably fit a battle with Grey and his household would have been an uncertain affair. Not knowing the layout of the house at all, he had doubts about his ability to get Pierce safely away. Nor did he know how much time he had but – and here came an encouraging thought – he did not think it likely that, given their chief's final mood, Albert or Charlie would report back to him to say that Cheyney and Pierce had been safely tucked away with a bedtime story.

But the carnage had to be cleared up. Cheyney quickly took stock of the corridor they were in, his hand resting all the time on Pierce's pulse, and his eye flickering back again and again to the man's face. Almost as in a hotel, there were doors on either side, two on one, three on the other – that last door must be the entrance to a bathroom.

His mind suddenly made up, Cheyney, Charlie's keys in his hand, went to the room that had been his cell. None fitted. He cursed, and then went back to Albert's body.

More success. He got the door open and the two bodies inside. A sort of macabre activity now seized him, and he wasted seconds over disposing the bodies in suitably challenging postures in the room. Then back to the other doors.

They revealed two bedrooms, of the same size and arrangement as Cheyney's own, one clearly occupied, one not. He hesitated, and returned for Pierce. Lifting Albert had been an especially difficult job, even for a very fit man. By the time he had Pierce safely laid on the floor of the unoccupied bedroom – so as to leave no trace – Cheyney was sweating and tired, and his head and face were again splitting open with the agony of Charlie's blow. He desperately wanted a rest, a drink, a smoke, another moment or two to think, but he had to force himself on.

Again, outside the door, he paused and listened. Nothing seemed to move in the musty interior of the house. Not the faintest sound, let alone a threatening one, came from that part of it which they had just left; and Cheyney flitted towards the bathroom.

Here he made another and, as it was to prove, priceless discovery. For there was yet another door. He opened it carefully and silently: it offered a narrow set of stairs, probably leading to the kitchen, almost certainly to another exit. More pieces of Cheyney's plan began to slot into place in his mind.

Back to the bathroom. Here was filth and chaos. The typical lower class crook is, in his home, if anything, an over-fussy creature: much of what he buys and provides is, if expensive, tasteless. But it is commonly kept in excellent order, and the successful member of the species is usually more efficient at hiring – and keeping – help to maintain it so, than is the honest citizen of equivalent, or almost equivalent, earning power. But a gangster's hideaway, or safe house, is rarely as kempt as a good pigsty.

Here were dirty towels in profusion, gallons – it seemed to Cheyney – of male cosmetics, a couple of ties, one thrown over the shower rail, another neglected on the floor, a grimy rim halfway up the hand basin. There was also a blue plastic bucket which, a sniff told him, had once contained disinfectant. This he filled with water. In it he dumped a towel; and then he sped back to Pierce.

The bruises and contusions on the Superintendent's face were grim. Cheyney, however, was less concerned with the pulchritude of his colleague than with his revival. It took all of five minutes before Pierce stirred and started in the crook of Cheyney's left arm.

'Christ,' he began.

'Quiet,' Cheyney said, calmly. 'Can you think?'

Another long pause. Cheyney had never before realised how fat Pierce's face was, and its pudginess as the head slumped on the broad chest lent a pathos to the marks he had suffered. Slowly, agonisingly slowly to Cheyney, Pierce began to think himself back into his own remote personality. Forcing himself, Cheyney waited in absolute stillness. Then:

'Yes. But I'm not all right.'

'What should we do?'

Another intolerable pause.

'Are they both dead?'

'Yes.'

Pierce tried to shift himself. Eventually, and with Cheyney's help, he got into a sitting position. He held up one hand after another and looked at it thoughtfully, flexing the fingers. Then he twitched his legs. 'I can't fight.'

'So?'

'Give me a gun and prop me up. Then get out of here and have the place raided.' There was a sudden twitch of energy and Pierce was almost himself. 'Now.'

60

Cheyney shook his head, gently. 'No, listen. I am going to leave you here. I have to. I couldn't promise to get you out. But I don't want this house raided yet. Listen.'

He spoke softly, quietly, persuasively, hoping that in his own pain he was making sense and that Pierce in his could understand his logic. Eventually, Pierce nodded. With Cheyney's careful help and an intolerant mutter or two, he moved himself across the room and under the corner bed. There he lay, humiliatingly facing the room, a gun grasped in his hand. He knew he must not lose consciousness.

Cheyney busied himself tidying up the evidence of their visitation. He straightened a rug, switched off the light, and returned bucket and towel to the bathroom. Then, gun in hand, he opened the stair door and began to make his way carefully down, treading on the very edge of the unclothed wood, where the creak, if there was any, would be least.

Again, he was lucky. The stairs led directly into a tiny pantry and hall. On his left was the kitchen; between him and it, a closed door. From behind it came voices, and the noise of bottles and glasses. He heard what he had most dreaded to hear, in a raised voice:

'Where the hell are those two fuckers?'

Cheyney did not wait. He was speedily and silently through the exit door and into a garden. He felt his way with his right hand. He had to be at the back of the house. Like a ghost he found his way around the gable end. Another door, a latch. Then he was out in the front.

The house gave on to a substantial frontal area, bigger than Cheyney had guessed. There was some, but not much, light for, though the lit windows of the house were curtained, a gleam shed itself over a gravelled parking area and path, across from which lay some indeterminate greenery. Everything now depended on whether Cheyney's physical and psychological guesses had been right.

On the physical he gave himself full marks. There were four cars in front of the house – a Triumph, a blue van, and two Capris. The Triumph, thank God, was both first in order of exit, and had a sunshine roof. Cheyney tried the boot. It was unlocked, and it contained a tool kit. He scrabbled. Apart from the usual accoutrements there was a small plastic pack of bolts, drills and screwdrivers. He was quickly through the quarterlight window, released the brake, got out, and began to push the little car slowly and carefully down the driveway.

He had to time things well, and he had to hope effectively as well. He worried ferociously about Pierce, upstairs, armed, but under a bed, battered and only semi-conscious. He worried about his splitting head and how it was affecting his judgment in the series of crazy chances he was taking. And he tried all the time to estimate distance and how far sound would carry amid the indistinct foliage surrounding him, and on so still a night as this.

Then he stopped. He opened the bonnet, jumped the ignition wires, and gunned the car engine once, and again, and again. Then he turned on the lights and shot it forward.

There was not far to go, and the gate was closed. Out. It was locked. The heavy gun in his hand, Cheyney sighted on the link of the chain by the padlock and fired. He swung the gates back, leaped back into the car and swung left.

Again luck – or the rewards of daring. He had clearly somewhat misjudged the area from the inside of the house, for it was evidently in some way rural, as his lights told him. Not fifty yards from Grey's front gate the lights showed, in a slight curve of the road to the left, a hedgerow bisecting two fields, and heavily overgrown. Out again to open the gate, and then a dreadful moment when the car wheels spun in the ruts, before he could get in safely under cover, and the gate closed again.

Then he was running back to the house, running in a swift, easy lope, every sense alive, his head suddenly clear and himself wholly committed to what lay ahead. At Grey's gate he paused. No activity inside yet. He was back through it and already in the thickets, now on his left, when panic-stricken torches came racing and bumping down the driveway. In concealment he saw Simmy, and another bigger man he could not identify.

'Jesus Christ,' said Simmy as his light fell on the broken lock.

'Back,' said the other man. 'Back to the boss.' And they both turned and began to run.

Cheyney could move in bushes and thicket more silently than most men, and more reliably than he could move in a city. But this territory was unknown, and he had to combine speed and relative silence – a silence made relative, fortunately, by the disorientation of Grey's men.

He almost kept pace with the two on the path who, unfit, wheezed their way back to the house. The door had been thrown open. In a flood of light Grey stood, unarmed, one man beside him with a hand gun, peering nervously into the darkness around him, gun jerking here and there, mind adrift. Cheyney's health had been restored by his exertions, and his confidence was remade by the contempt he instantly felt for somebody surrounded by arms, but in fear of two fugitives.

About Grey himself though, there was no fear. He stood, hands in pockets, nothing about him moving but his head, which cast this way and that as though he were a hound on scent. Cheyney could not hear the exchanges between Grey and Simmy and his companion, but the big man was attentive, and did not seem censorious. Then, from the tunnel of light behind him came two more men – toughies,

Cheyney could see, but not so tough now, out of their depth in the face of some nameless terror loose about them. One spoke, and almost in a scream.

'Nothing, Mr Grey, nothing anywhere. Only Albie and Charlie.'

As though to restore order in his disordered ranks, Grey raised his voice:

'Right. No time to clear up. They'll be back with the cops. We're all on the run now. Get your gear and get out.'

No general could have given a more masterly retreat order, nor one so quickly obeyed. In a second the front of the house was empty, the light poured out on nothing, and Cheyney was running towards what he had selected as his best bet, the van.

If it had proved no good he had planned to wound Grey and scare the others. But the back door was open, and quick inspection showed the thing full of odds and ends – some planks, a piece of furniture – and blessed sacks. In a moment Cheyney was burrowed under the sacks, up against the driver's seat, further concealed by a table, itself hooked loosely to the wall of the van with straps.

For the next minute or so there were confused noises outside, then the van door opened and Cheyney curled his finger round the trigger of the gun. Something heavy was dumped into the back of the van, then pushed – shoved – further up its length. Gears crashed, and the cavalcade began to move with at least, Cheyney noted, two people in the front of the van. The van bore right at the gate – Cheyney could not tell where the two other cars had gone – but, as they took a further right-hand turning, and fell for seconds under the dim glare of street lamps, he shrank back, not for fear, but because, inches from him was the same sight of Charlie's dead and bloated face as had been seen by him before, by a dead wall in a dead house.

On they drove, and on and on, at what must have been risky speeds, given even their known cargo and the alarm they must have expected to be out for them, but with many twistings and turnings, avoidances and reversals. Cheyney could compute time accurately in his head, but the jerky diversions of the van and his own pain, now returned in full measure and exacerbated by the dead presence lying in intimacy beside him, were throwing, he felt, his judgment. As near as he could make it, an hour had passed before the van pulled to a stop. There were a few inaudible mutters, and a passenger was gone.

Cheyney was disappointed, but not markedly so. He could hardly have expected that Grey himself would be in the van, nor that by concealing himself he would unravel a mystery. He was concerned only to extend and broaden the shaft of light on his problem that he had seen playing about it that evening. If, as he suspected from the day's experience, Grey was adrift from the underworld – though no doubt still feared – and with a limited number of desperate allies, then any one of those allies would lead him further than a mass arrest followed by interrogation, even supposing such could have been organised in the time and circumstances available.

In so far as a man can be said to be content when lying in the back of a smelly van under sacks and being taken to an unknown destination, and nose to nose with the distorted face of somebody he has just killed, Cheyney was content. He had a name – Quex – and the knowledge that Quex was fat, for Grey had referred to his fat legs. There was a woman in the case, and Pierce, who would now certainly survive, might well know who she was. There was no further link with Tommy – with a stab of guilt Cheyney realised that he had scarcely thought of Tommy or his parents since lunch. But, if pieces were not exactly falling into place, there was at least movement, and Clement

Grey as well as Allen Cheyney was on the trail of Mr Quex.

Cheyney had almost gone into a reverie when he realised that the van had slowed. It was as though the driver were seeking an address. Another safe house? Then it stopped. Cheyney dared not raise his head, but the old, familiar friendly excitement stole over him. The driver got out, and he heard the clanging of a gate. Then silence. Perhaps gone to open a garage, perhaps to awaken a friend? Then the driver was back and, sure enough, the van was manoeuvred into a garage.

Cheyney heard something, a voice, but so low he could not distinguish any words. His only understanding was of a note of surprise. The driver's door had been left open and he could hear continued exchanges. They must, he thought irritably, be keeping their voices deliberately low. He shrank back into his protective covering, in case anybody chose this moment to shift Charlie's carcass. While he was doing this his mind left the conversation, and he was only vaguely aware of some scuffling. Then there was silence.

Cheyney gave himself ten minutes by his mental clock and then slowly began to flex his muscles, rid himself of cramp, and get ready to leave the van. Another five minutes had passed before he raised his head, but he could see nothing. Then – three or four minutes more – he got to the rear door and found he could open it from the inside. Another three minutes to find that it could be opened silently, and to get outside. There was certainly nobody in the garage. He moved to his left, round towards the driver's seat, aware all the time that there was something in the atmosphere that ought not to be there, that he could not fathom, through his pain and concentration.

He stumbled against something, and bent down to feel it. A wave of nausea and horror came over him, for his

66

hand, which came away sticky from the thing, told him that here was another body.

And then he knew what he had not been able to fathom. It was the cloying odour of a woman's perfume.

CHAPTER EIGHT

News of Tommy

Simmy had been – according to the police surgeon with the pudgy fingers – knifed *beautifully* in the back. Cheyney, having found a torch in one of the recesses of the garage, identified him and then, step by step, room by room, explored an already abandoned semi-detached house in Fulham. There was nothing he could do in his brief survey except establish the emptiness of the house, and the presence, in one of the rooms, of the perfume of the woman who had probably, in the garage, disposed of Simmy. Three bodies in a night, he thought bitterly, as he sat down to telephone the Yard, by three different hands; and although he now had more information, he had a feeling that there was altogether too much light in the affair. He could hope only that the latest burst of action indicated that somebody, somewhere, was getting worried. But if he and Pierce were close to anything, he had not identified it. Nor had what seemed like the brilliant idea of tagging along to Grey's caravanserai led to much.

These defeated thoughts were in Cheyney's mind when he let himself into his flat, to a howling, leaping welcome from Bruce, at half-past three in the morning. There was a note from Nelson, and cold food in the fridge. Tired, hungry, and hurting, Cheyney took Bruce for an early walk in the misty darkness; showered, shaved, and sat down to his salad with a large whisky. He had left the 'scene of the crime' men at the Fulham house and returned to Surrey. He had been, after all, right in locating the house where he had been kept prisoner in the Home Counties. He had seen Pierce, unconscious again after the effort of phoning his people, taken to hospital for care. He had recovered his possessions, and especially his Palgrave, now a memorable trophy of a memorable tale, and had been driven home by the police.

While he ate, Cheyney discharged all his problems from his tired mind. He was back in his haven, his dog at his feet, his food and drink before him, and Nelson somewhere in the building. When he had finished eating he retired to his study, intending to think, but fell fast asleep before the fire, to be woken at seven by the prowling Nelson, with salve for his face, black coffee and bacon and eggs.

Nelson was a man as big as Albert, but without any of Albert's disfigurements. He had been in the Navy, and still walked with a roll. Years before, when Cheyney had bought the little block of flats in which he lived and, though wary of personal servants, wanted somebody reliable and capable of all purposes near him, he had accepted Peter Graham's recommendation and taken on Nelson. His only worry since then had been the degree to which he had become dependent on the big, soft-spoken Somerset man with the dreamy, almost vacant face, muscles of iron and a brain which, though somewhat limited, was none the less perfect within its sphere. Communication between them was almost perfect, though almost invariably non-verbal. Nelson was Grimaud to Cheyney's Athos.

After he had had breakfast Cheyney telephoned the hospital, to find to his surprise that Superintendent Pierce had already discharged himself. On his mettle now, Cheyney called his car and went down to Whitehall. To her eternal credit, Miss Levison showed no reaction to the weal across his face as she welcomed her customarily disciplined and impeccably dressed employer back to his office. Cheyney went through his pile of documents and appointments in an hour, waiting with concealed impatience for some news from Pierce. Again, pride and mutual respect forbade a call once Pierce had returned himself to duty. By eleven Cheyney had completed his outstanding business and asked all security departments to check out the name Quex. Within a further half-hour he had delegated all outstanding business to Major Galbraith, spoken to his Minister, and told Miss Levison that from lunchtime onwards she could expect him when she saw him. Irrational, unjustified though the feeling was, it was none the less very strong with him: developments were coming.

By half-past twelve Cheyney, though he was not quite purring with satisfaction, had at least something to brood on. He had learned that the intelligence services he had called on had knowledge of one Hubert Quex. The surname was so unlikely as to be almost certainly unique, and the man had a political background of sorts. The great difficulty was that he had disappeared from sight some fifteen years before.

Most of the information Cheyney had had before lunch was computerised, part of that news agency service that friendly intelligence agencies provided for one another on request and as a matter of course. Quex was the son of an old Northumbrian family – the surname, Cheyney was astonished to find, was ancient in that part of the country. He had made a fortune in South Africa – not necessarily by dubious means; any new arrival in the sphere of large money drew the attention of those Cheyney had consulted. Then he had gone to ground, to emerge later in South America, as the proprietor, in alliance with various more or less rapscallion regimes, of substantial silver mines. And there, in 1960, everything had stopped.

But there was another piece of information available to Cheyney before he went to lunch. It was not computerised, and it came to him with the authority of his opposite number in Tel Aviv, Dan Ma'oz. Cheyney had more trust for the general ability of the Israeli intelligence services than had most of his Western counterparts, who were inclined to distrust their enthusiasm and their fixity of objective, characteristics which Cheyney found encouraging. For the judgment of Colonel Ma'oz, however, he had no scepticism whatever; and Ma'oz informed him that Quex was believed to have been the financial adviser to the Paraguayan government for a decade until 1970, and to have emerged from that backwater of the Third Reich with massive resources. And that was the last that even Israeli sources had heard of him, emplaned from Asunçion to Mexico. And, thought Cheyney, his inflated spirits suddenly down again as he looked at an indistinct twenty-year-old photograph of Hubert Quex, it need not even be the same man: the only certain thing in common between this and Clement Grey's Quex was that they were fat.

After Miss Levison brought him his sherry – for, though she did not know it, the last time in a long period of field action – he stood again gazing from his window as he had gazed two days previously, when he was recalling Peter Graham. He had a feeling that something around him was breaking, that he was looking again into Charlie's dead face, that all the security and order and fanatical discipline of his office, in which men dead in action – whether on our side or theirs – were mere details that Cheyney recorded on the chessboard, had given way to something else. He had not, he realised, experienced activity of the kind he had endured the previous day for a very long time; nor had he expected to have to face it ever again. He was indescribably weary and he wished violently, as before he had wished theoretically, that he had resisted the importunings of a few years ago and gone to do what he knew best in his home.

Miss Levison had been told that Cheyney would take Superintendent Pierce's telephone call.

'How are you?'

'Well.'

Pierce was exactly himself.

Cheyney said: 'I have something for you.'

'Yes?'

'The woman.'

'Oh,' said Pierce, 'Grey's old girl-friend. Her name's Lavinia Dawson. We've known about her for a long time. Her perfume stinks. I expect you smelt it around that garage.'

'Yes.'

Fellowship, Cheyney thought, was impossible with Pierce. After all they had shared the previous day the man was still robotic. Imaginative in many ways though he was, Cheyney did not understand that he himself projected to his own staff very much the same impression of personality that Pierce conveyed to him.

'I want,' said Pierce, 'to talk to Sir Peter again. I would be grateful if you could come with me, but I would like to talk to you first.'

An hour later Cheyney and Pierce sat in a private room at the Owl in Westerham and had their first meal together. Somebody had done a miraculous job on Pierce's face for, though he was bruised, and the corner of his mouth had been stitched, he had nothing like the dreadful aspect of the previous night. Neither greetings nor commiserations were exchanged, and Cheyney began by telling Pierce over the whisky what he knew of Hubert Quex which, when he put it before the flat appraisal of his colleague, seemed very little, and what there was of it notional.

'Aye,' said Pierce, 'I begin to think of it all as political, not commercial.'

'One thing before we talk,' said Cheyney, his curiosity rampant. 'How did they take you, yesterday?'

'In my own car,' said Pierce. 'And now I had better tell you why I want to see Sir Peter Graham.'

Averse though he was to paper on his desk Pierce was not, Cheyney saw over the next hour and a half, opposed to either food or drink within his reach. He put away enormous quantities of the first and substantial of the second, while filling Cheyney in on what he knew and guessed, the only faintly comic feature of the proceedings being the necessity of speaking out of one corner of his mouth. Finally, over a huge helping of pie, he summarised:

'Here is what I know and believe. The woman Grey meant had to be Lavinia Dawson, who goes under the stage name of Lavinia Duchene. She's a stripper and a whore, but different from the common in that she really enjoys her work. The Duchene is not completely false, because at some time in her life she enjoyed a couple of years of very expensive French education. The story is that it was paid for by her father, and that when he died it had to stop. I've seen her strip. Compared to some girls who do it she's nothing in particular, but she can do things with the customers.'

Cheyney frowned at the photographs Pierce had given him, showing a woman slightly overweight everywhere except around the middle.

'Grey fell for her. That's unquestioned. He was the biggest thing around in her world, and he went overboard. Now, here's something I can't get quite right. Clement Grey is not the kind of man to share his girl, but Miss Lavinia certainly went on living on her own, and she never, so rumour has it, stayed a single full night at Grey's place. That kind of rumour, in that kind of world, is usually reliable.'

'And you have no idea where she is now?'

Pierce shrugged. 'I think I may have. But let me finish about her and Grey. You know that our underworld is like a complicated crossword – like the one in *The Spectator*. It's a criss-cross over a criss-cross, if you see what I mean. Some of the criss-cross refers to territory – Boss A can't enter the ground of Boss B without invitation. Billy Hill's legacy that is. But there's a criss-cross for jobs as well. A peterman from Lambeth may get a commission in Birmingham, but his local boss – in this case the mob still hanging over from Richardson and Kray in Brixton – needn't know and doesn't much care. Grey was unusual because he was the only territorial boss – based in West One – who was a job expert as well. He kept his own patch quiet and lawful, more or less, so we found it impossible to hit him; and he hired himself and his team out elsewhere. He was so good and so hard and so bloody tough that other territorial bosses swallowed what he spewed out, and they never felt they *had* to do anything about it because Grey was first and last a job man – he didn't want anybody else's patch.

'He was at the top until we took him for the Oldfield job – maybe for about seven years. For the first six or so of those, and for the ten while he was climbing, it was often said that he was queer. When he had women he beat them unmercifully and paid them off, but there were no permanent attachments, except for one Albert Rogers.'

Only the use of the word 'one', Cheyney thought, suggested that last night had even happened: even then it might be the pompous circumlocution of a policeman.

'Miss Lavinia made the difference. She was queen of Grey's stratum' – Pierce, who had been gazing into his glass, looked up and diverged – 'I use the word because it so often happens that folk live in a neighbourhood without knowing at all what goes on in another level of

74

that neighbourhood, of West One. When she was in West One she was gangster's moll number one, and the moll of the number one gangster. But she drank in other patches, she slept in other patches, and she stripped in other patches. She had, for example, a favourite haunt which was a dirty little pub in Camberwell Green Road, and she took off her clothes there often enough. And Grey let her get away with it. More important, he got away with it.'

'By that you mean?'

'Nobody in Grey's profession can afford that sort of abuse for very long. But he was too feared, y'see, and too well-connected job-wise, and too unambitious for territory, for anybody to take advantage of whatever it was he felt for her. Then, when he got taken, she disappeared. She must be the woman he was talking about last night. She's got to be.'

'And you think she killed Simmy?'

'She must have. That was an address we had for her earlier, and that perfume you found there – that's hers, not marketed in London.'

'And you know where to find her?'

Pierce's head moved half an inch to the right and half an inch to the left. 'I know a couple of places outside West One where she might be. You have to remember that we never had any interest in her, professionally. We never kept a track, nor tried to.'

'And you're holding something back.'

As Pierce grinned Cheyney was vividly reminded of the shocked and battered man who had killed somebody in the upper hall of a neglected house the previous night, and who had slid into unconsciousness with a defiant joke about middle-aged coppers.

'Well, I told you she liked to wander. Just before the Oldfield job – a month, in fact – she acquired, through her agent, an assignment to strip at a Cambridge May Ball.

Tommy Graham organised that ball, and he took her out to dinner before it.'

Pierce drained his glass and Cheyney said, with a sinking heart:

'We'd better see the Grahams.'

CHAPTER NINE

News of Grey

It was too late in the year, and too cold anyway, for Maria Graham to give Cheyney and Pierce afternoon tea on the lawn, but they had it anyway, in a large and pleasant studio-room, the huge french-windows of which – clearly an alteration in the walls of the old redbrick house – looked over her and Peter's carefully tended gardens. She was imposing herself on disaster, but there was everything tender, and nothing dominant, about her.

Cheyney she kissed warmly on his arrival: to Pierce she offered a friendly hand. Peter Graham was far more unhinged than when he had left Scotland Yard. He fussed, he pottered, he offered whisky, he tried to take the men into his study – falling back, when Cheyney made it clear that this was very much to be Pierce's show, on mutters.

'I think,' said Cheyney, 'that Mr Pierce would like to talk to you both.' He then recalled the horror of hearing Graham and himself discuss the weather in the Arches, for his old friend tried to take him away by himself, 'just for a moment, y'know.' And Cheyney remembered that, at the Yard, Graham had warned Pierce and himself that he might not be altogether reliable in any pursuit of his son.

Cheyney was heart-stricken for Graham, and irrationally angry that his friends might appear in a poor light before Pierce, who stood bruised, silent and watchful before all the chatter in the Graham hall, that centre of all that Peter had spoken of to Allen Cheyney when they had lunched.

From disaster, Maria Graham rescued her confused male company. In her presence Cheyney had always felt that he had not changed his collar, that his hair needed cutting, that something about him was askew. Yet, he would never have felt the need to ask her permission to smoke between courses, as he invariably did. And, now, seeing her for the first time in years, he sensed in her a terror as deep as Peter's.

As the four settled on opposite sofas in her studio Cheyney looked at her. She was, to his taste, a perfect beauty. Only one other woman he knew could excel her. Her face was a perfect oval; her eyes blue and calm; her smile genuine and infectious. But she was forty-five at least, and, superimposed on the facial lines of her age were extra notches of worry, born, Cheyney guessed, since Tommy had vanished. The major question was whether, like Peter, she had gone so far in grief that she wanted to conceal anything that it would help Cheyney or Pierce to know; or whether she was prepared to tell them about her son.

At the Arches Peter had said that his son's colouring was the same as hers. Her hair, though, Cheyney saw as she bent, was copper, not blonde. And she frowned as her head went down. It was the frown, Cheyney thought, of somebody unmanned and in trouble, who did not know where to turn or what to value, but who was going to fight.

'Mr Pierce,' she said suddenly, just as everybody – or at least Cheyney and Graham – thought there were at least some more silent formalities to be gone through, 'you know perfectly well that I answered questions from your people for six hours, and from you for another two. You would not have come with Colonel Cheyney' – she nodded to him – 'unless there was something new. Is Tommy dead?'

'No.'

Pierce had spoken – flat, unemphatic, metallic. But

Cheyney's mind was racing away, and wondering about empathies between the minds of mother and son.

Cheyney watched her. She had finished pouring, finished her distribution, sat back to look at Pierce. A third set of lines had suddenly imposed themselves on a face that, however beautiful, was worn. It was her moment of maximum weakness, and Pierce went instantly into the attack.

'Your son, Lady Graham,' he said, without moving or hunching himself, or appearing to prepare physically in any way for his assault, 'hired a sleazy stripper to perform for his students, and took her to dinner. I know that. Did you?'

It took two seconds before Peter Graham jumped. 'Allen,' he shouted, and started for Pierce.

None of the other three moved, but somebody had to say something, and Cheyney said it:

'Sit down.'

'No,' said Maria Graham, and her left hand reached along the sofa to her husband, whether to give or receive comfort Cheyney could not tell.

'Is it important?'

'Yesterday,' Pierce said, 'I killed a man, and Colonel Cheyney killed another. That may well be the sort of thing Cheyney does quite often, but I have never done it before. Also, Lady Graham, before I killed that man – his name was Albert, by the way – I was told by a man who had beaten me up rather badly that he wanted to get hold of a woman; and that woman was your boy's whore.'

Oddly it was Peter Graham who replied.

'Pierce,' he said, very quietly, 'neither my wife nor I are fools, and we are not going to be bullied or horrified. I asked Allen to help me find my boy, but I understand perfectly well, and Maria understands as well, that both of you have a big job in hand. Of course it distresses us – you can see how much – to think that our son might be involved in anything as big and horrible as Allen described to me in your office. But that doesn't mean it will break us; or that your vulgar description of a student prank will wring something from my wife you wouldn't otherwise have got. We have, Superintendent, tried to help you in every way possible.'

It was the best speech Cheyney had heard from Peter Graham. But, he suddenly realised, a scar had been inflicted on his own friendship with the Grahams that would probably never be wholly removed. Intellectual as well as emotional instinct told him there was nothing to be achieved by Pierce's storming tactics, both because they simply would not work on a woman like Maria Graham – even if she had something to conceal – and because, quite simply, there was nothing to conceal, the Grahams being as puzzled and helpless in their personal problem as he and Pierce were professionally. But he, Cheyney, was miserably trapped: he could not interfere with Pierce, and he could not help the Grahams; but he was convinced that the whole interrogation was a waste of time.

But Pierce showed no sign of defeat, and none whatever of embarrassment. And there was no doubt, Cheyney thought, that his stamina was unbelievable: he had taken a terrible beating, been in hospital and, on his own implied confession, been deeply marked by the killing of Albert. The marks of his suffering were on his face, but he showed no impatience, no energy, no emotion, no vindictiveness. Only his words, lashing, cruel and coarse, marked any commitment to attack; and once they were uttered it was almost as if the silent, plump, detached man in the corner of the sofa had not – could not – have uttered them.

He now set about Maria Graham in detail. He told her – hardest blow of all, this – of her husband's confession that he might not be reliable at all stages of the investigation. He told her that the coincidence of her son having hired a particularly notorious and well-connected stripper to appear at a May Ball, and the subsequent disappearance of the same son in circumstances which suggested a connection between Tommy and Quex simply could not be borne. And he implied in every sentence that there had to be – just had to be – some piece of knowledge that Tommy's parents, wittingly or unwittingly, were concealing.

'Your husband,' he concluded, nodding to an again broken Peter, 'told me that there was a growing estrangement between him and the boy, between the boy and him, but not you. If there had been some change in the boy, something that would lie behind any new associations he had been making, you must have seen it.'

But he could not create guilt in Maria where, patently, none existed. She answered readily enough:

'Of course I saw that Tommy's relationship with his father was changing, and it upset me, but I thought it was something that would pass.' She paused and, abruptly, went on the attack.

'Have you children, Superintendent?'

'No.'

'Married?'

'No.'

Maria took no advantage of either of these negatives. 'My husband has always been a more disciplinarian – no, that's the wrong word, more *demanding* – parent than I am. Of course, as you have seen, I am distressed and worried and shocked that, as you seem to know, Tommy was consorting with people like this woman. In the back of her mind every mother knows that her boy may go wild at university, do things that she would regard as, well, unsavoury; and hypocritically or not, most mothers prefer to keep their vague knowledge at the back of their minds. That is what I have done. You have made me face the details of Tommy's activities, and I am very hurt and, well, dirty, because I've had to do this. I also see that you – and, I suppose, Allen here – are right in thinking that my son has got himself into very deep water. I haven't come to terms with any of this yet, Mr Pierce; and, if it's any satisfaction to you, this interview will plague my mind for years.

'If Tommy is alive, Mr Pierce, and if I see him again, I'll never be able to forget what you've told me and the way you've told me. But I have nothing to tell *you*, and I am neither deceiving you nor protecting my son.'

She leant forward, and freed her hand from that of her husband. Her face was now very deeply distressed, and she looked much more than her age: but she was also even more beautiful than before, even more indomitable. Cheyney remained convinced that there was no treasure lying behind the wall Maria Graham had erected about herself, and that Pierce had been mistaken in supposing that there was. But, in any event, his storming of that fortress had been disastrously unsuccessful. There was a question Cheyney wanted to ask, but Maria had not finished:

'I have this much faith in my son, Mr Pierce: I believe him incapable of deliberate evil. But Peter and I have seen a great deal of evil and mania loose in the world, and I couldn't swear to you that my son did not in some way become a part of it. But my belief in him, Mr Pierce, is not protective. It is so strong that I would not lie to you about him, and certainly not with Allen Cheyney here.'

Pierce, Cheyney sensed, had already acknowledged defeat. But he had one last try:

'Lady Graham, the proximate cause of the last dispute between your son and your husband was a drugs charge laid against Tommy by the local police. He was found in possession of, and high on, marijuana. I take it that, for the purpose of this discussion at least, you are not challenging the overwhelming probability that the police charge was accurate and would be proven?'

She shook her head.

'Nor that you would agree with me that the taking of that kind of drug in quantity, and the possession of it, is a most serious business – not just a serious offence, but something bad and wrong in itself?'

She shook her head again.

'And you still say that you had noticed nothing remarkable about Tommy, nothing beyond a casual and teenage disaffection?'

'I still say that.'

'Maria,' said Cheyney, and his voice was as gentle as honey, 'twice in this conversation you have referred to Tommy as dead, or to the possibility that he may be dead. Can you tell me why?'

She faced that fence as steadily as the others.

'I don't know, Allen. Ever since he left the house I have expected to hear that he has been found dead.' She wrapped her arms around herself and looked out into the garden, and suddenly the cheerful room was cold, and dank, and threatening. 'There is some sense in which he is dead.'

Cheyney, wondering what Pierce thought of this as a technique of investigation, feared that the Superintendent might bring his bludgeon to bear on a manifestation of maternal metaphysics. But Pierce merely stood up to take his leave. Yet Cheyney went reluctantly, for he somehow felt that they were at the heart of the mystery, at least in so far as it concerned the disappearance of Tommy Graham. He was astonished and gratified to be kissed as warmly by Maria on leaving as on arrival, but not surprised that Peter's farewell was as perfunctory as it could be. They left – he and Pierce – Cheyney felt, a stink behind them.

They had come from London in Cheyney's car.

83

'Back to the city,' asked Cheyney when they got in, 'to the Yard?'

'Drop me at Liverpool Street Station,' said Pierce. 'I'll get a train to Cambridge tonight, and go over the Tommy Graham trail there tomorrow.'

And that was the last word spoken between the two men between Kent and Liverpool Street. Pierce had brought a briefcase full of papers and he went steadily through them between the Graham house and the railway station. Cheyney sat back in the corner of his seat, wretchedly convinced that he had somehow blundered in everything. There was a breach between himself and Peter Graham that he could understand, and a breach between himself and Pierce that he could not. He suspected that his one question to Maria was regarded by Pierce as a way of taking her off the hook, but he remained himself convinced that that challenge and response had got them further than all Pierce's bullying. Only, he could not explain why he thought this, nor how his thought had worked out.

The confident conviction Cheyney had had that morning that things were suddenly going to start to move was almost wholly dissipated. There was too much light and too much darkness in the whole business. Cheyney had the ineradicable feeling that he was up against the darkest and most mischievous business that he had come across since the war, but he had no idea why he had that feeling, and no clue what to do about it. He wished, he wished desperately, that he could recreate with Pierce that moment of macabre comradeship that had existed between them in the death-filled corridor of a Surrey house the previous evening, but he could see no way to do it. From now on, he felt with a desperate sense of loneliness, he and Pierce would go their separate ways.

It was well after a reasonable dinner hour when Cheyney's driver pulled into the second scruffiest major railway station in London. Pierce put his papers back in his case and climbed out. Then he turned to Cheyney, the door still open.

'I don't,' he said, 'like my job any more than you like my way of doing it. Goodnight.'

Cheyney sat in the car for a few moments and then told his driver to take him to the Wig and Pen. He dismissed the man there and went in to a chop and a bottle of claret, during which he mulled over the whole business again, seeking connections that did not exist, and answers where there were none. In the bar on the way down, his stomach full of grease and wine, he met an old friend, and stayed for a couple of whiskies and a little reminiscence. More lonely and cold within himself than he had been in years, he went out into a now rain-sodden street and called a taxi to take him back to his flat.

Cheyney's spirits revived in the taxi, and he promised himself a therapeutic walk with Bruce and a cold shower before a good night's sleep. His brain spinning with weariness he walked through his little hall, entered the living room and saw Bruce stretched before him on the carpet.

Clement Grey rose from a chair by the fire, pointed a gun at him and said:

'Good evening, Mr Cheyney.'

CHAPTER TEN

Nelson Intervenes

Blood started to Cheyney's eyes and to his head and he went across the room after Grey.

Whatever Grey could have done with the gun Cheyney, given a few more seconds, would certainly have killed him. But Grey did not fire: he moved back and got the table between them, genuinely anxious and outraged.

'Hold it,' he shouted, 'would I kill a dog? The animal's only drugged, man. Keep it cool.'

Slowly, very slowly, Cheyney came back to himself, while Grey stood, both worried and wary, by the fireplace. Cheyney went to Bruce and went down on his knees beside him. He verified that Grey had told him the truth: Bruce was breathing heavily and sluggishly, but he was alive and unharmed and, as Cheyney stood up, he noticed the little feathered dart, withdrawn from the dog's flank, which lay on the table.

'I'll just frisk you,' Grey said almost apologetically.

Cheyney went to his sideboard, put his hands palm down on it, and leant forward as Grey went over him. He was breathing heavily and painfully and, even after Grey had withdrawn, he lay stretched there, bringing himself together. Then he turned around and faced Grey. Again, as for a moment the previous night, he seemed to have the ascendancy: his close-cut red-grey hair was tousled, and his stiff, striped suit pompous. Underneath his tan he was pale with the shock he had received: but his eyes burned steadily with hatred at this invasion of his fortress.

'Hey,' said Grey uneasily, 'I came to talk. I wouldn't hurt a dog, I promise you. I came through that window there' – he nodded across and Cheyney saw a shattered pane – 'and popped him one. He'll have a hangover, I guess, but he's not hurt. Guaranteed to keep him out till breakfast time. But he's not hurt. You believe me?'

'I believe you.'

But Cheyney still seemed not quite over the shock. He had turned to face Grey, but he now turned back to the sideboard and lifted a decanter of brandy. As though to signal a truce he held it up to Grey, but the man shook his head and pointed – again almost apologetically – at a full rummer on the arm of his chair. Cheyney turned his back again and his hand shook as he moved the decanter towards a glass. He put it down, mopped his forehead, gripped the raised back of the sideboard so tightly that his knuckles showed white, poured himself brandy in a tumbler, added soda, and walked coolly enough over to the fireplace to take the seat opposite Grey.

There was a ghastly chattiness about that man tonight. 'Brandy and soda,' he said. 'Now, it'd take class to get away with that nowadays. Gentlemen, I'm told, take their brandy neat: I do. But that's a new fashion, isn't it? In the nineteenth century, the history books say, brandy and soda was a proper upper-class tipple.'

'I had gathered,' said Cheyney in a tone which mixed weariness, contempt and nervousness, 'that you were interested in history.'

He genuinely could make nothing of Grey. The previous evening the man had been all power – mad power, sane power, vulgar power, but all power. Tonight, in spite of the menace of the gun, he was more like the eager but deprived child in an under-privileged East End school, anxious to impress a sympathetic teacher with what he had learned, keen for approval and beneficence. Truly,

Cheyney had met nothing like him before. But his interest in the character was faint and flickering: cold detestation, as for an insane but thoroughly obnoxious animal enemy, was imposing itself on all the other moods of the day.

'I told you,' he said, 'that I would kill you for what you did to Pierce. You realise, I hope, that you have doubly signed your death warrant by breaking into my home?'

He was still maintaining his dominance of the situation. An unimpassioned observer of that weird conversation would have realised that Grey would not shoot Cheyney down, unless Cheyney went for him; that Cheyney would not go for him; and that Grey understood what Cheyney meant, and believed it.

But Grey still had something to say, and it was a variation on one of his themes of the previous night. He said it with a preface, but, as he spoke, a number of his personalities – the eager, tough kid, the hardened killer, the insane man of power – dropped away, and he spoke directly and simply:

'You hit me hard last night, you and Pierce. Simmy's dead?'

Cheyney nodded.

'You know by now about Lavinia? She killed him?'

'I believe so.'

'I've lost the others too. What I told you last night, that they didn't care about consequences – that doesn't count after the kind of beating you gave me last night. I'm finished, Cheyney, even more finished than I was when I got put away in the nick. There's only me, myself, left now. I'm not appealing, I'm stating a fact. But, by Christ, I'm going to leave a lot of damage behind me.'

'What have you come here for? Do you propose to try to damage me?'

Grey shook his head.

'I came to deal, but first I'll tell you something.'

He paused as though to collect his thoughts. The gun was on the right arm of his chair, and his hand was resting carelessly on it, but there was such a tension in the air between the two men that, careless though Grey's hand looked, Cheyney would never have dared to spring across the space between them. As though to signify his acceptance of the, at least temporary, situation between them he sank back into his chair, and his left hand stole up over his head to grasp the other point of the wing of the chair behind his head. His attitude said that Grey could speak with complete freedom, and without threat.

'When the Oldfield trial was going on,' said Grey, 'a chum of mine in Glasgow paid me a visit. He said he had been asked to recommend a man who could break Oldfield out. I said, no dice, no way, I never got involved in security cases. He said his principal wasn't a Russian but an Englishman, and that he wanted to meet me. I said he could come and see me. He did. He's a huge guy, Cheyney, huge and fat and old and filthy. He offered me a half a million, whatever way I liked, to burst a bloody sergeant out. But it wasn't the money that made me take the job. It was the way he talked, the feeling I got from him that I couldn't do it. That made me try. So I got Oldfield out. And I buggered myself as a result.'

He relapsed for a moment into silence. He was so rapt that Cheyney dared not interrupt the silence, dared not fracture this most unexpected of reminiscences. The fire that Nelson had piled up was seeping away, but he did not want to distract from this fraught interlude by so much as throwing another log on it. He had not wavered from his determination to kill Grey, but this intimacy between them was, he saw, precious.

'How much did Pierce tell you about me and Lavinia?'
'Enough.'
'He took her off me, Cheyney – that first night. I don't

know how he did it – he must be all of twenty stone or more, and I doubt if he could get on top of a woman without killing her. But I always let her go her own way, as long as I was number one, so I didn't even see what was happening. It wasn't till I was locked up that I saw it. That's why I'm after them both.

'Now, Cheyney, you see what I was after last night. Maybe I wasn't very diplomatic about it. But I've never learned the need for it till now. When it's too late. You and Pierce between you lost me my last men last night. But don't think because I'm on my own I can't put the frighteners on people, or that I can't get Quex, for me and for you.'

Cheyney spoke.

'I can't deal with you, Grey. Not because you're a villain, but because you killed coppers.'

'Bugger that. I don't want to sit down in an office with you and your pal from the Yard and draw lines on maps and go off with the Sweeney to catch Quex. Just give me what you've got, and I'll get Quex. I have one lead myself, with what you've got I can put it together. I only want twenty-four hours. After that you can do what you bloody well like.'

Cheyney was going to speak again, but Grey forestalled him. At last, they were down to the irreducible personality of Grey, and it was a desperate spectacle.

'I'm mad on that woman, Cheyney,' said Grey, in a terribly quiet, resigned voice. 'She burns me. I'm forty-two. It's never happened before, and I won't live long enough for it ever to happen again. You'll get me, Cheyney. I know you will. I'm out of my division in going up against you. I knew that yesterday, even when I could get the drop on you. Even if I got you, your lot would get me. You'd do it better, but Pierce would do the same. I was mad to do the Oldfield job, and I think *he* couldn't have persuaded me if she wasn't there. So I'm not asking for a pardon, Cheyney, I just want a chance, I want a chance to do your job for you.'

'No,' said Cheyney, and then suddenly, 'What do you know about your Lavinia and a young Cambridge boy?'

Grey's head shot up. 'Nothing. Are you giving me information?'

'No. If you don't know about it, you can't help me. I'm not even sure how important it is.'

A log in the fire cracked and broke into its carbonate parts. This time Cheyney did move, down to his knees to stoke up the fire with green, long-burning logs that shut out the hard, rainy night, shut out slumbering, drugged Bruce, shut out a mad conversation between two desperate men, shut over, for a second, as a lifted rock restored covers a squabble of competing, cannibalistic insects, all the dreadful implications of a mystery Cheyney did not understand, and one part of which Grey understood all too well. A truce between enemies on the battlefield was coming to an end, as both heard the distant sound of the big guns.

'Grey,' said Cheyney, 'I cannot deal with you. *I* cannot. Don't suppose that I won't deal because of Pierce and his coppers. I wouldn't, even if Pierce would let me. And I have nothing to give. My hand is empty. You say you have a lead. Pursue it.'

He had never seen such desolation as there was in the eyes of the other man. Big, brown, luminous and threatening, they were now terribly lonely. Everything Grey had ever done or dared, mad, bad and vicious as it all was, was wiped out in that look. One moment full of meaning and of possibilities now long dead existed between himself and Cheyney.

Everything Grey had said ran through Cheyney's mind, and especially his hardness when telling Albert and Charlie to take himself and Pierce away to the desert that would have been the following morning; but especially also his genuinely indignant and even frightened assertion that he could not harm a dog. Yet, in spite of the congruence between what Cheyney was about and the vengeance Grey wanted whatever it cost, nothing was possible between them. Even Cheyney's loss with Peter Graham and Grey's loss with Lavinia Dawson could not bring them together. There was too much blood. Grey postponed the moment of parting. He drained his brandy and fiddled with the gun and looked deep into Cheyney's revived fire. 'Nothing, then,' he said at last.

'Nothing.'

Bleak and cold Cheyney's word dropped into the room. There was nothing he could ever give to anybody, and nothing at all in his lucid moments he could ever want to give to this creature, half-mad killer, destroyer, thug.

'You don't have to tie me,' Cheyney added. 'I won't tell anybody you were here.'

Grey nodded. He lifted his powerful frame out of the chair and walked through the door, strong but sagging, burdened with a consciousness of things as they were, of relations between people, of power and of personality that, if he had ever even guessed they existed, he had crushed in his limited path.

But Cheyney's hand for the evening had not yet been fully played, and the blank cards he had shown Grey were not the only ones he had available. He gave Grey the length of a cigarette before he rose, inspected a mumbling Bruce, and went to the bathroom to shower. Clean and refreshed he put on dark clothes and a black sweater and sat down again by the fire. Years had dropped away from his face: he was young again, sharp, eager, and on the scent. And he had two things in his head: when he had leaned on the back of the sideboard he had signalled Nelson to follow

Grey; and Grey had said that he had one lead of his own. In his present mood, Cheyney reckoned, he would follow it up that night.

Cheyney had smoked ten cigarettes and thrown the end of each into the dying fire he no longer had the interest to revive again before his telephone rang.

It was Nelson. Cheyney listened carefully and repeated an address. 'Ten minutes,' he said.

Then he carefully lifted the still slumbering Bruce on to a sofa and went out into the night, pausing, this time, for a gun.

CHAPTER ELEVEN

The Hand of Quex

The feeling Cheyney had had that morning – that things were moving – was now fully back with him. His tiredness had gone completely, and his disappointments, aggravations and self-doubts had vanished completely. He was, as he went rapidly and lightly down the stairs, an almost perfect fighting machine.

Pierce was in some Cambridge hotel, sourly, sorely but unemphatically reflecting on the failure of the day's effort, but determined, so Cheyney guessed, to try the following day on some of Tommy Graham's friends the techniques that had failed on his mother. The Grahams were tossing restlessly in Kent, worried, damaged, hardened, perhaps even estranged. Lavinia Dawson was still in the flood-tide of some weird self-indulgence, and Hubert Quex was being complacent.

It was odd that Cheyney felt this. Quex to him was still an unknown quantity, merely an idea, a combination of something Grey had said, and something the computer and Dan Ma'oz had thrown up. But he was, as Cheyney raced down the stairs, a real and palpable, fat and dangerous, human being. Grey was playing his last card, lonely, despairing, uncaring, cut off by his experience from Cheyney, whom he might in different circumstances have reached, by two killings.

His power lost, from all that he had built up since he had stolen his first handbag, because of his irrational passion for a woman. He had no hope of survival. But he was, perhaps, the one thing that could break open a six-month-old puzzle, precisely because he no longer cared what happened to others or to himself. He was out there, somewhere in this rain-sodden and windswept London night, with a gun and by himself, playing the only card he had left.

Before he went to the garage for his own car Cheyney stopped, and sniffed the auspices of that awful night. He lit another cigarette in the shelter of his porch, and in the light of the unblinking lamp that burned from dusk to dawn in the tiny porchway of the block. Then he walked slowly through the sweeping gusts of rain to the garage where he kept his Bentley. Perhaps too much emotional strain, more than he could recall on any job for eight and a half years, too little sleep, and too many contrasting styles of work and experience, had made him light-headed. But his slowness, his carelessness, were fatalist: wherever Grey was playing his card Nelson would wait for Colonel Cheyney.

A few minutes later Cheyney came up St James's Street into Piccadilly, and a moment later he was around Eros. It was well after midnight, but the ranks of the huddled mass of youthful, drug-ridden, pathetic and anti-pathetic youth which normally frequented this centre of a once-great city, though thinned, were still there in force. In his present mood, going on to something desperate, Cheyney was inclined to be more sympathetic than censorious. But he recalled lunching with a friend in St James's only a week previously. He sympathised warmly with the graphic picture the friend, a painter, had drawn of the insidious flux between the horrible commercialism of all the neon that surrounded and dominated Piccadilly and the wretches who thought they were defying these symbols, but still grovelled beneath them. This, Cheyney reminded himself, was the ground that Clement Grey – and probably Hubert Quex – cultivated; and their cultivation was all the more

95

fruitful for the conviction of their victims that they were, in some fashion, free of exploitation. Again, as he had felt earlier in the day when Pierce had assailed Maria Graham, Cheyney believed he was close to the heart of things. Could Tommy Graham, picked up with marijuana in his possession, be a part of this rabble which, in a different mood, Cheyney would want swept from the streets with power hoses?

Cheyney parked his car in Golden Square and walked back to ruined Piccadilly. The rain had stopped now, but the night offered no promise of cleanliness: it was heavy, and sordid, and overcast, and before long the huddlers would have to flee, or huddle closer, in the face of gust after gust of rainwater discharged from the sky with all, and more, of the force of a power hose.

Before he reached the chemist's shop which stayed open all night, and which was already infected by muttering, prancing, scratching youngsters, some of whom might well have had National Health prescriptions for whatever it was they needed to give them peace, Cheyney was accosted three times: twice by youngsters who thought that his slow, careful, disciplined figure was that either of a homosexual pimp or a drug-pusher – Cheyney was not clear which – and once by a girl who wanted money, and would have given anything for it. Then, at the corner, there was the huge, reassuring Nelson.

Nelson never hunched himself in against rain or weather, or any other experience. He now stood at ease, and no kid, it seemed to Cheyney, approached, or ever had approached him.

'Well done,' said Cheyney.

'No, sir,' said Nelson. 'I was very shocked when I heard your bell. I thought nobody could get past me.'

'Grey could get past anything,' said Cheyney.

'What now?'

96

Nelson, towering over Cheyney, his bulk and his sweater and Naval jacket enveloping, as it seemed, his employer, the cruel arch of his nose pointing, indicated a side street.

'Up there's Moran's club,' he said, 'and your man went in there nigh on twenty minutes ago. By himself. There's nothing nastier than Moran's.'

In the mood he was in Cheyney found it natural to wonder when and how Nelson gained his knowledge of the nastier sides of London life, for there was about Nelson something that suggested, not just force, but an irreproachable respectability. However, he knew, not Moran's, but the reputation of that place. He knew, also, that Nelson was waiting for a decision.

Suddenly, Cheyney remembered Grey's reference the previous evening to the Peninsular War; and he recalled a remark the Duke of Wellington had coined. 'In for a penny, in for a pound,' he said. 'Let's have a go.'

The two men, one huge and rolling, one tall and thin and sharp, walked in step up the side street. The people who then backed Moran's club owned the whole of the building, of which it occupied only the first and second floors. Thus, the complete ground floor was an area of protection. You could get into the little entrance hall by ringing the door bell; but you could see no fun from there, only a sharpfaced little man in a booth, and two bored-looking heavies standing about him. The little man's job, for which he was highly paid, was to assess the commercial value of anybody who wanted to come in; that of the heavies to ensure that anybody who did not meet his standard was kept out.

He looked at Cheyney. 'Sorry, sir, we're closed.'

In the most friendly way Nelson reached past Cheyney and hauled the little man over the counter of his booth and out to the floor. Cheyney would not have had the sheer strength to do that. But it had the great advantage of taking the little man away from the bell which he would have used to signal upstairs that there were difficult customers below.

Meanwhile, Cheyney was dealing with the other two. The fundamental thing about West End heavies is that they never expect to be taken at their word, except by people whom they recognise, like other heavies, or the police. The latter they treat with a certain sulky respect: with the former a battle is a purely notional affair. Since Billy Hill, one side has assessed the other and dominated or given way. A West End heavy can earn a very good living looking tough to customers without ever adding to the scars he earned when he was a boy. It is a quite exceptional experience to come across a team like Cheyney and Nelson, genuinely out to hurt, genuinely desperate.

'Good evening,' said Cheyney, his conversational opening wholly in keeping with the strange mood that had come to him. He kicked one man straight in the stomach and, in almost the same fluid movement, used his cigarette case to open the other's brow on a line parallel to his eyes. As the first man doubled, Cheyney's left hand took him by the hair, drew his head in, and hit him straight in the face with his right knee.

Then it was Nelson's play. The booth-keeper cast lightly into a corner, Nelson took the man half-blinded by blood and chopped him over the collar. 'Dear me,' he said, as he looked for a second on the other victim of Cheyney's mayhem, and then he took all his pain away with the smooth, cutting heel of his right hand.

The terrorised man sitting in the corner, who had seen many raids, and many rumbles, was – because his life and profession depended on such understanding – appreciative of what followed. Nelson took out a torch and shone it on the ceiling. By its light Cheyney disconnected the lamp over the door which invited purse-careless passers-by to try

Moran's. Then Cheyney took the torch, and Nelson wrapped all three victims of the assault in wire.

That little man had seen so much that there was a certain objectivity about him which overcame terror.

'Jesus,' he said, despite his discomfort, 'are you Clem's new boys?'

A warning note sounded in Cheyney's head but, in spite of his new mood, he was confused by all that had happened during the day, and he ignored it. It was absurd, he thought, this invasion of what was essentially Pierce's territory, and how easy it was. The ruin he and Nelson had created in a moment in a West End club, in an area of London the police clearly preferred to leave alone had, in its inception, nothing like the quality of opposition he had seen in Yugoslavia, or Korea. This was child's play.

'Is Clem upstairs already?' he asked, thinking himself clever, and adopting what he thought was the kind of tough manner the little man would respect.

But, all his life that little man had had to balance one force against another – he had no other possibility of a life that would earn him five thousand a year tax-free – and he had had to work all the time on his wits. The volcanic force that was Cheyney he wanted to propitiate; but he had not the wit to do it properly.

'Yeh, Clem went up,' he said, and he wanted to add to that; he wanted to say that Clem had gone up and that he and the heavies had been left. But Cheyney swept him aside.

'Good,' said Colonel Cheyney. 'Right, Nelson.'

Nelson was already positioned by the door to the stairs, and he had already cut off all of the electrical apparatus available to the booth-keeper. They went up a narrow set of stairs, Cheyney first, Nelson second with a gun, and came into another reception area that was bare, and went on, into a bar.

The sight was extraordinary. There was a huge rectangular room, against the right wall of which was a semi-circular bar. The bar was directly in a line with their point of entrance. It glittered and tinselled, and had everything in it that a late-night West End drinker would want. But, it was different because, his back to them, Clement Grey threatened the three barmen and all the customers alike with the gun that lay beside his brandy and soda.

There were perhaps thirty customers, and all of them had been crowded into the other end of the room. There were a few moneyed visitors among them, frightened, out of their depth; a few of Grey's own class, but not of his level; a few bewildered people, like the little man downstairs – like head-waiters in terrible restaurants trying to conceal by their bounce the appalling fare they had to offer. The – clearly senior – barman was speaking as Cheyney came in.

'Christ Almighty, Clem,' he said, 'whersit gonna getcha?'

'Who cares,' said Grey, and then Cheyney, making yet another dreadful mistake, intervened.

He walked forward very quietly. 'That will do, Grey,' he said, in his quietest voice. And then, with an absolute clarity of conviction, added, 'Which is she?'

He swept the middle-aged, inconsequent, well-off, guilty, hard with his eyes. It is moot whether Grey respected him, or noticed the careful Nelson with a gun trained on him; for Nelson had no imagination. Anyway he avoided the question.

'Cheyney,' he said, 'look at them. They've been in my clubs for ten years – more – without knowing what makes their fun. Look at them, Cheyney, look where they come from.' He broke into that croon he had. 'Leeds, Bradford, Halifax, Huddersfield. They told us that in school, Cheyney. They told us that in school.'

He picked up his gun, and drunkenly sighted it. The

100

huddled thirty shrank back into themselves. Every eye was, not on Grey, but on Cheyney, uncaring. 'Which is she?' said Cheyney again.

A couple of women wept, and their make-up cracked, a couple of men tried to bluster – they had been talking, twenty minutes before, about the washing machines they had come to London to sell, or about bed. All, suddenly, saw Cheyney, in his last confrontation with Grey, take the upper hand for the third time.

Cheyney walked past Grey on the left, and Nelson followed him in a further loop. Grey, Cheyney could see, was not only playing his last card, but was terribly, viciously, suicidally, drunk. To the tatterdemalion now behind him, however, whimpering as they were, Cheyney was the man in control.

He almost whispered: 'Which is she?'

Grey gestured with his gun. Cheyney turned to note, briefly, a woman in green, starting for a door. Then the door through which he had himself come, opened. A youngster from the street stood there, with something in his hand. He was bearded and be-jeaned, and he cried, 'All power to the people'; and then he threw.

Nelson jumped on Cheyney. A second later, when the bomb had caused carnage all round, Cheyney was remembering his failure to see the significance of the fact that Grey had been allowed to go upstairs in the club, without any change in the guard.

Meanwhile, he knew that Grey was dead, and that he was looking up into the dead face of his beloved Nelson, whose bulk had kept him alive.

'Quex,' thought Cheyney, and passed out, determined to be revenged.

CHAPTER TWELVE

The Minister

For the second time that night Cheyney returned home. But on this occasion it was dawn when he at last let himself, shocked, dispirited and heartbroken, into the living-room of his flat, where the glasses he and Clement Grey had drunk from only a few hours before still stood in their places, rimed and unwashed.

Bruce had recovered: but it was a sadly puzzled, and obviously very uncomfortable, dog who returned to his master's half-hearted greeting. The room was cold with the chill of death on it, and barely an ember survived in the grate. Cheyney sat down and put his head in his hands. He knew, and he felt that Bruce knew too, that nothing could again be the same here without Nelson. A whole chapter of life was closed; a great force in the balance of their existence had gone to a heartless, mindless, mass killing, and everything in life seemed made of ice. Bruce, as though sensing what had happened, forgot his own discomfort and pushed his nose in between his master's laced fingers, eventually licking the tears from his face.

Then the telephone rang.

Almost automatically, Cheyney picked it up, dully uninterested in who might be calling. In seconds, however, his mind was completely alert. He had neither reached his present position, nor been able so often to defy those placed in authority over him, without having built up all through his career a network of friends, who could be trusted over and over again to sustain and support both his actions and his beliefs. His caller was Tom Morgan, the duty officer at the Department that night, and he had gone out to a public telephone box to make it.

'Allen. How are you? I'm dreadfully sorry about Nelson.'

'Thank you Tom. What's the trouble?'

'Well, you, old boy, I'm afraid. In fact, it's not just that you're the trouble, you're in trouble.'

'Let's have it.'

'As duty officer I have to call you in an hour, and summon you to see a Panjandrum at ten. The word is you're off this case.'

'But it's a Yard case. They asked for our help.'

'I think you'll find the heat is on friend Pierce as well. Sorry, Allen.'

'Very good, Tom. Thank you for calling. I'll remember it.'

'I know you will. Good luck.'

Flagrant disregard of rules, thought Cheyney, with his first touch of humour in hours. But there was no doubt now that he was in serious trouble. In previous crises he had always had somewhere to point, some piece of information that would allow him to defy an immediate superior, and go above the man's head. Cheyney's own ruthless integrity, his refusal ever to scheme for position or honour, combined with the extraordinary success of his operations, had so far kept him well ahead in the games-playing stakes of Whitehall. But, if he was to be pressed now, he had nothing. He had even, he thought, alienated Peter Graham; he had irritated Pierce; and he had been at least part of the cause of too many deaths.

And now he had to think. Whatever his instructions were going to be, the only thing that mattered was to revenge Nelson. In his shocked state Cheyney had blurted out his ideas about Quex to the Scotland Yard man at Moran's, but he could see he was being listened to sympathetically rather than seriously. Bombing in London was now so regular an affair that, short of blaming the IRA, nobody would listen to a conspiracy theory. What the Yard officer had written down would, Cheyney knew, be the first document on somebody's desk that morning, and none of it had been very considered or thoughtful. If what he had to face in the course of the day was merely another Whitehall scrap, which he could arrogantly ignore, Tom Morgan, who was a sane and common-sensical man, would not have telephoned him. As, a mute Bruce following him, Cheyney helped himself to another whisky, raked the ash in his dead fire and started it up again, looked at his mauled face in the mirror, a retreat which might be the basis of an offensive was being planned.

To two convictions Cheyney clung. Mr Quex – whoever Mr Quex was – had been responsible for the club bombing. And Mr Quex wanted to get, not just Clement Grey, but Colonel Cheyney. Neither conviction was really supported by hard evidence, but Cheyney, for all his discipline and routine essentially a man of imaginative fits and starts, had never doubted the quality of his own judgment. To his first proposition he now added another: Mr Quex had a remarkably effective intelligence system. How far and to where it penetrated Cheyney did not know. But if he was himself to be put under the kind of pressure that would isolate him from most of his own sources of knowledge and influence it was possible that he might plant something in the jungle he was leaving behind that might attract the attention of the only predator he was interested in.

An hour to the moment after his first call, Cheyney's telephone rang again. This, of course, was the formal, monitored call.

'Colonel Cheyney? One moment please, I have the Duty Officer for you.'

'Colonel Cheyney? Major Morgan. Will you log this call,

104

please. The Secretary of State would like to see you in his office at ten this morning.'

'Any indication?'

'I'm sorry, sir. I am merely passing the message. Will you acknowledge, please?'

'I acknowledge.'

Then, because even so brutally official a call did not need to be inhuman, Tom added, 'I was very sorry indeed to hear about your troubles last night, sir.'

'Thank you, Morgan.'

'Good morning, sir.'

Not just a Panjandrum, then, but the – in Cheyney's world – second biggest Panjandrum; and, further, a man for whom Cheyney had only the deepest and most active loathing. But on this occasion, he knew perfectly well, the gun with which he was faced was too big for him. He picked up the telephone and ordered his car. Then he took a last, long look around his flat, and spent a few minutes in silent memory of all his escapades with Nelson. Then he cleaned up, showered, shaved, and cooked breakfast.

With an hour to get to his Whitehall appointment, Cheyney dressed, even by his office standards, in a remarkably impeccable and conservative fashion, telephoned his brother, and arranged for a suddenly acutely worried – there was a remarkable fellow-feeling between the two men – Mark to collect Bruce in mid-morning and look after him until further notice.

All Cheyney's thinking had been done while he fed himself and watered his dog. Even Bruce's distress at what he sensed in the atmosphere he almost ignored. Cheyney's energy had gone into contemplation, not just of what he now called the Quex affair, but of every other paper that had crossed his desk for a year. And, spurred by exhaustion, grief, and desperation, he had divined a clue. He rang Peter Graham.

He was not warmly received. Accursed as Englishmen with attachment to forms, their estrangement had to be made more manifest by the exchange of a series of politenesses. But Cheyney could now take only so much of this, and he had to attempt the route direct.

'Peter, listen. Let's, please, drop the niceties. For various reasons, none of which I can really explain except by saying that I am in very serious difficulties, I want you to go to my house in Scotland, by yourself, please, and wait for me there, however long I take. I want you there by yourself. Will you do that?'

There was a long silence.

'My guess,' said Cheyney, 'is that we'll sort it all out there. But I have to know now whether you trust me on that.'

Quemoy, Cheyney thought furiously, remember Quemoy. Then Graham proved his peerlessness.

'Of course,' he said, 'where is the blessed place?'

Cheyney gave Graham the number of his London solicitor and then himself immediately rang that long-suffering individual, who had vicariously taken tenancy in his life so often in the past.

'John? Allen Cheyney. Will you do two things for me, please? Shortly a friend will telephone who wants to spend some time in Galloway. Make sure he gets my keys, will you, and all the information he needs about Loch Hill. Then, John, I want you to put this London place on the market. You already have my power of attorney. Will you do that immediately, please?'

'My dear Allen,' said John Anstruther, 'I read the morning papers, and I see that a certain Colonel Cheyney – of, so far as I can see, no fixed abode – behaved very gallantly in an affray involving, probably but by no means certainly, the Provisional IRA last night. Are you in terrible trouble, my dear fellow? You can have large sums of money without selling, you know; and this is not, in any case, the best time to attempt to dispose of property. Perhaps we could lunch today.'

'I want rid of it, John,' said Cheyney, 'and quickly, please. And, no, I'm sorry, we can't lunch.'

'Suit yourself. Good luck, Allen.' Anstruther sounded disappointed.

One more call, Cheyney thought, and it might turn into a series. He rang Scotland Yard. This action was both the biggest of the risks he proposed to take, and the best way of testing the strength of the force building up against him in Whitehall. Superintendent Pierce was, he found, already in the office, but he was with the Commissioner, and unable to speak, even to Colonel Cheyney. He could ring back, though, in ten minutes.

When, after fifteen minutes, Pierce had not telephoned, Cheyney tried again. He was perfectly aware that, in doing so, he was failing to respond to the most simple, the most beautiful, and the most heartless of all bureaucracy's devices, the unreturned call; and he was aware of the surprise of the secretary on the other end that he had failed to take the hint.

'Get me,' said Cheyney, using not only his name but his manner, 'Inspector Matthews. I have a very important appointment very shortly and there is a message that must go to Mr Pierce.'

The surprised and affronted girl got him an aggrieved Matthews. The word, clearly, had filtered down, and Matthews was not averse to seeing an important somebody get the brush-off. But neither was he anxious to make a mistake. With luck, Cheyney thought, his message would get through to Pierce as the assertive last play of a man on the way out, but with enough suggestion – given his reputation – in it to cause some stirring.

'Matthews? Good. I want a message to get to Pierce.

Part of it is confidential between the three of us. All right?'

'Very good, sir,' said Matthews, as he rolled his eyes and reached for a pad.

'Ah, splendid,' said Cheyney, enjoying playing the Colonel for the first time in years. 'Tell him, will you, confidentially, that I have some bother with my people, and that I suspect that we won't be able to work so closely together in the near – got that, the near? – future. But tell him also, will you, that I have a very promising line on Tommy, the drugs, and Scotland.'

'Tommy,' said a disbelieving Matthews, 'the drugs, and Scotland?'

Fifteen minutes later Cheyney's driver arrived, and found his boss in unexpectedly good spirits, reading the morning paper accounts of a bombing the previous evening in a Piccadilly night club.

Thus, Cheyney went to see his Minister.

CHAPTER THIRTEEN

Cheyney's Capture

'Take the day off,' said Cheyney to his driver, as he got out of the car under that most implacable of Whitehall's monstrosities, The Ministry of Defence, 'but give me the keys.'

Accustomed to the whims of his tiresome boss, Jones, who had never formed any sort of relationship with the Colonel, saw, stretching ahead of him, a riot of beer and darts and passed over the keys.

Whether in trouble or triumph Colonel Cheyney never did things by halves. He showed his pass to the security officer but, after that, allowed no rigmarole to hold him up. On the fifth floor, almost swinging his umbrella, he brushed aside a personal and a private secretary and told the latter:

'My appointment is for ten o'clock precisely. It is ten o'clock. Show me in.'

Her Majesty's (then) Secretary of State for Defence was a lawyer. He was a middle-sized man with a resonant and attractive voice, trained partly in court, and partly at the hustings. He had what – to be fair to him – was, in a Labour government, the most impossible of all jobs, for no more than a handful of his colleagues cared about his brief, while a sizeable number worked actively to have it abolished. He had built up an improbably large ego at the Bar, and had, at one stage, even thought of himself as a possible Leader of the Party. His present job, he knew, excluded, in so far as he discharged it with any degree of conscientiousness, any possibility of that consummation. He was, therefore, both embittered and frustrated, and felt himself unfairly ground between the millstones of the Defence Staff on the one hand, and the Labour Party National Executive Committee on the other. It was unspeakably irritating for him to have responsibility, under the Prime Minister, admittedly – but the Prime Minister never appeared to be available when difficult matters were on the agenda – for Colonel Cheyney and his freebooters. Nonetheless, and this was something Cheyney did not see at all, Simon Collins did try to do his best.

'Well, Cheyney,' said Collins, fussing with a pen tray, 'that was a nasty business last night.'

'Which business, Secretary of State?' said Cheyney, in his most impossible mood.

Collins matched him. He was a man with a very flat face, who had never quite overcome the barrister's tiresome habit of sticking his thumbs in between shirt and waistcoat. He no longer did that, exactly, though his hands, thumbs extended, waved about somewhere in the region of his armpits. But he was no fool.

'Cheyney,' he said, 'you and an officer of the Metropolitan Police Department have been chasing what you both consider to be a conspiracy for six months or more. In all that time neither of you has come up with a shred of evidence. Now, that is of no matter so far as my Department's subvention of your budget is concerned: we are always prepared to pay for research. But I draw the line, when a police officer kills a man, when one of my officers does the same, and when my same officer, the following night – the very next night, Cheyney – precipitates a bomb incident in which thirteen people are killed and more than a dozen wounded. You must see, first, that you make my position impossible when I am trying to get a reasonable defence budget through and, second, that it does not become middle-aged Security executives like yourself to become involved in night club brawls to no purpose.

'I should add,' said Collins, looking directly into Cheyney's eyes, 'that your counter-intelligence outfit is *ad hoc*. Created by the Prime Minister it may have been. But I have to pay for it, because of some strange notion of the Prime Minister, great and good man that he is, that there should be a security department independent of the Home Office. You know, Cheyney, that every penny I give you comes from the Chiefs of Staff, and that you failed to make lunch with one of them the other day?'

Cheyney was all velvet and hate. 'Have you recalled, Secretary of State,' he said, 'that on both of the occasions you mention we were – or I was – attacked? Neither Superintendent Pierce nor I sought out hostilities. Does that not suggest that we have not been wasting our time for the last six months?'

Collins, very savagely, hit back, and said, 'I understand you have a personal interest in all this?'

'If you mean that one of our most promising lines of enquiry was opened up through a personal contact, yes. But I would like to remind you that Peter Graham came to me, not just because his son was missing, but because of something he found in the boy's possessions. It was that which started Superintendent Pierce and myself off, and it was after the connection had been established that the violence began.'

'I dispute that, Cheyney. In so far as the violence was not precipitated by either yourself or Pierce, it began with the escape from gaol of Clement Grey. I have responsibility, thank God, neither for the police force nor for security in Her Majesty's prisons.'

'Do you want my resignation?' Cheyney asked evenly.

'Oh, don't be a bloody fool, man,' said the Secretary

of State in genuine bad temper. 'Look here' – he waved a file at Cheyney – 'this is a record of your work for the last five years. All of it is good. Some of it has been quite brilliant: I give you that, however much you and your people try me. But it is espionage and counter-espionage, Cheyney. It is patient, boring, methodical work, enlivened occasionally by the opportunity to exercise flair. And you have agents in the field to do your dirty work for you. I repeat: I cannot have middle-aged, desk-bound Civil Servants involved in skulduggery.'

'Do you recall,' Cheyney asked, stubbornly, 'that it was you who sanctioned the establishment of Pierce's and my team?'

'I have the paper here,' said Collins, not without a certain sense of triumph. 'I, and my colleague, the Home Secretary, sanctioned the establishment of a liaison team, solely on the ground that one link in the chain you and Pierce were establishing had a security aspect. A liaison team, Cheyney, not a licensed murder squad.'

The trip-hammers of temper were already beating beneath Cheyney's temples, but he made a last effort to avert what he knew was coming.

'I will readily confess,' he said calmly, 'that a good deal of what Pierce and I have assembled may well seem to you to be tenuous in the extreme, and that even if there is something there it might be more the responsibility of the police than of my department. There is, however, no doubt in my mind that the basic structure of whatever we are up against is criminal, not political. But there is the devil of a lot of politics in it somewhere. The Oldfield episode by itself would be proof enough of that. If it were not, the slogan shouted by the bomb thrower last night would by itself be enough. You were kind enough' – Cheyney was incapable of not flavouring the phrase with a touch of contemptuous sarcasm – 'to refer, flatteringly, to my flair. I would go farther. I have never, and my record shows that I have never, been wrong in estimating the origin, nature and size of a threat which has any relevance to my Department and its work. I am not wrong now. Whoever Mr Quex is, and whatever his organisation, he and it represent a major security risk.'

Collins looked at him carefully, and said, very quietly, 'Cheyney you are an insolent and intolerable bastard.'

It was almost a moment of contact between them. For a brief moment Collins was surprised at what he had said, and pleased by it. For the same moment he had Cheyney's respect. Then Collins, his sloe eyes cast down, his voice firm and flowing, set seriously about removing any embarrassment.

'As you know, or should know, perfectly well, there are two kinds of politics. One exists under the technical term, security. It is a matter of spying, subversion, and the actions of unfriendly powers. That is your job, and I would never seek to instruct you in it. But there is also, Colonel Cheyney, the system – the kind of politics according to which this country is governed – by people like me, Cheyney, not by people like you. We live, so far as the second kind of politics is concerned, in a particularly frenetic and anarchic age. Of course, both the saboteurs whom it is your duty to apprehend, and the crooks who are Pierce's business, will try to, and frequently do, use intellectually and morally dislocated people, and especially youngsters, in the pursuit of their own ends. As a citizen you may fairly say that my kind of person – the politician – has done too little about this and has done ineffectively what he has attempted. But, as a public servant you must accept it when I lay it down – as Pierce must accept it when the Home Secretary lays it down – that incidences of moral and intellectual dislocation are not your business, nor are they part of the material you work with.'

The Secretary of State had not finished. He raised a hand to prevent any intervention by Cheyney and pushed a box of cigarettes towards his guest. Then he went on:

'It is quite absurd to suggest, either that the disappearance of Admiral Graham's son – who appears to have been no better and no worse than many young people today – or the shouting of a slogan before a bomb is thrown, is automatically evidence of the kind of activity in which you are professionally interested. It is no time since the child of a senior minister was found guilty on a drugs charge. The immediate victim of your bomb was a common criminal, one who has been engaged before in many underworld battles, and I would be far from surprised to find that a criminal rival had chosen to dress up this dreadful act in political colouring.

'For most of your life, Cheyney, you have been a public servant of distinction. But unless the distinctions *I* make are observed, you and your kind – and I include Pierce – will become dictators of thought: you will presume to evaluate, in terms of whether or not it presents a threat to the interests you are charged with safeguarding, what people think. Whereas the true task of you and the police alike is to apprehend people for their actions. In the present case everything that happened lies in Pierce's not in your field, though I happen to know that the Commissioner intends to take Pierce off the case.

'One final word: the dictatorship of thought which I suggest is a very real internal threat, is not, of course, something that Colonel Cheyney would ever attempt. It is lesser men, the lesser men who might follow in Colonel Cheyney's path, that I fear. And at present, in the delicate state of politics, and bearing all the distinctions I have made in mind, the Ministry cannot afford *this*.'

With a lawyer's gesture he faced Cheyney with a smudged *Daily Mirror* photograph taken the previous evening, of Cheyney in conversation with a police-man.

'Do you know,' Collins added, 'how many reporters have been inquiring about you? And that it has taken me most of the night to prevent, without the use of a D notice, further coverage of your interesting life in the newspapers. It will not do, Cheyney; it will not do.'

Cheyney felt a dreadful, indescribable weariness. Nothing showed through the mask of his face, but his legs ached and his head swam. He saw faces, while there was only the blur of the man relentlessly pressing him from the other side of the desk. He saw Tommy Graham's face – Tommy as he had last seen him, and Tommy as he was in the photograph Pierce had procured from his parents. He saw the dead face of Charlie, the hard, high face of Grey, the shattered face of Peter Graham, and the beautiful face of his wife. He saw Bruce's shaggy, worried face, and another dead one, that of Nelson. He saw them all in the kind of brief, waking nightmare that comes to a man shattered by sleeplessness, exhaustion, tragedy and hate. He saw the faces swim across the backdrop of his flat and, behind that, a huge, amorphous, fat, indistinct face of a man he was going to kill.

'I will resign immediately,' he said.

'No, you will not,' said Collins. 'You are far too valuable when your mind is not distracted by personal and ideological considerations. And you know perfectly well how much damage a resignation would do, not only to this Ministry, but to your Department. It would be bound to get out, and I could protect neither you nor your office. A resignation would be fatal to all the good work that you have done, and all the people who depend on you.'

Cheyney's mouth was dry and his tongue seemed huge. 'Leave,' he said.

Collins' face began to clear. 'Provided you assure me there

will be no free-lance activity, certainly. I think a month's leave would be ideal.'

'I'll go,' said Cheyney, childishly pleased with his cunning in avoiding the assurance, 'to my house in Scotland.'

'Splendid,' said Collins. 'Now, what about some coffee? How is the house getting along, by the way?'

'One more thing,' said Cheyney, 'the distinctions you have just made – in the present climate they are false.'

Collins hesitated. Then, with the humorous impatience of the politician who has gained his negotiating point and is anxious not to prolong dispute, but to engender good will, waved a hand, called for coffee, and asked Cheyney to tell him about the house.

It was nearly twenty minutes before Cheyney, a docile Cheyney, who had shyly and unwillingly discoursed on a home that had long been in his family, had fallen to ruin, and had been restored with four years of patient, if intermittent work by himself, left. Then he went across the courtyard to his own office, smiled sweetly at Miss Levison, cleared his desk and departed, leaving her with the conviction that he was up to no good.

But Cheyney's mood was anything but mischievous. The darkest depression of many a year had settled on him, and only the reflexes trained over thirty years kept his face unclouded, his back straight, and his stride brisk. The dispositions he had made – the guess he had made – seemed so futile, so thin, so inadequate, both against the forces that he suspected – felt – lay just beyond his vision, and against the destructive and planned indifference of his superiors.

For the moment he had nothing to do. He drank a cold beer at opening time in the King Charles and then crossed Whitehall, struck through the Horse Guards, and made for St James's Park. Of all the places in London that he loved, this he loved best. It was a public place, and increasingly tatty, like all the best beauties of London. But he always felt intensely private there. Only once had he taken any companion, save Bruce, to his favourite spot, or adopted in the sight of anybody who knew him his favourite posture, leaning on the little bridge with the pelicans to his left and the ducks below him, gazing back at Whitehall and beyond it to the point where the delicate and involved structures of the Embankment roofs traced the lineaments of a mysterious, hidden city in the morning sky. His mood being black he noticed, as often he did not, the ugly structure of the Shell building behind those minarets of such elaborate tracery, testifying to an Imperial experience of grace, beauty and order; Shell representing the intrusive latecomer marked by greed and a willingness to ignore where it did not annihilate the fusion of architectural styles over which it loomed.

Seldom, in recent years, had Cheyney so articulated his feelings and, when he turned back from the parapet of the bridge he was in a trance, mixed between depression and exaltation.

The mood explains why he took several seconds to take in the presence of, and identify the raven-haired woman and the stiff, gangling boy with the vacuous eyes and the dribble at the corner of his mouth. On the bridge in St James's Park Colonel Cheyney had found Tommy Graham, and met Lavinia Dawson.

CHAPTER FOURTEEN

Hubert Quex

Cheyney's first realisation was that she was not, in any obvious or generally understood sense, beautiful or seductive. Her hair, black and shoulder length, framed a face squat rather than aquiline, almost Asiatic, of the cruder sort. If she possessed beauty, then it was of a very different sort from the beauty he had been admiring in Maria Graham the day before. Her figure, too, was unremarkable: she was short, heavy-breasted, and square. But there was something in her eyes, and something about her stance, intensely provocative, and intensely cruel. Cheyney had never known what to expect if he ever met Lavinia Dawson, but he recalled Pierce's respect, and Grey's agony, as her personality gusted over him.

'Mr Quex,' she said, as though she were a nanny introducing an especially fondled child to a friend of the family, 'thought you would like to see Tommy.'

Her left hand lifted from the boy's shoulder and caressed his face – short, squat fingers, ringed, clumsy and taunting. Far from being warm, it was a cold day: Lavinia Dawson was wearing a heavy, camel-hair coat. But Tommy Graham was sweating. His trunk was rigid and his legs stiff, but his arms, themselves seemingly brittle, dangled loosely from his body as though they had little connection with it. He wore a sort of grin – a rictus of the face, rather – and gurgled and dribbled. Yet, his gait aside, he was a well-proportioned boy, and should have been handsome. Another face rose before Cheyney, the face in the photograph, of a careless, muscular, independent youngster. His beloved park, and his beloved spot in that park, were suddenly cold and chill and ruined.

But Cheyney, shocked out of his reverie, would nevertheless never allow himself to be outfaced.

'Good morning, Tommy,' he said, 'it's a long time since we've met, but your parents are worried about you.'

The woman was surprised, and something almost like intelligence flashed in the boy's eyes. 'How,' he said, slowly, with difficulty, almost unintelligibly, 'are...' And the rictus and the dribble took over. Cheyney noticed, suddenly, that Tommy seemed not to blink at all.

'What part had you in this?' Cheyney snapped at the woman. Bereft by what he had seen of the rest of his sophisticated response, he had gone right back to his own, natural, trained, domineering type.

'Piss off, Cheyney,' she said, facing him squarely, her solid little figure opposed to his, lean, pin-striped, the essence of the secure. 'Look behind me, and look behind yourself. Mr Quex has a man at each end of the bridge. He wants you to pay him a visit, and if you try anything *you'll* still get there, but your precious Tommy won't.'

With an almost infinite amount of care Cheyney took out his handkerchief and wiped his face, looking steadily, coldly, all the time down into her eyes. He had never been more lost. He did not bother to look behind, for he could see, over her shoulder, the first of the guards she had told him were there. In the middle of London – within almost shouting distance of hardened gunmen like Galbraith or Morgan – he was completely and irrevocably trapped, not just physically, but morally. He did not doubt his own ability to take the bridge at a spring, surprise, confound and probably kill Lavinia Dawson's escort. But whether his computation of his own powers was accurate or not he would certainly, as the woman saw, have to sacrifice

Tommy. And he would have to do that while Tommy's father was already on his way to Scotland, on Cheyney's instructions.

A shaft of cold, autumn sunlight came out and bathed the little group. A couple of preoccupied folk hurried past the three men, the woman, and the boy on the bridge. On Cheyney's left were Buckingham Palace, a barracks of soldiers, the expanse of the park. On his right was the architectural vision in which he had been drowning himself. Between him and it was a politician who had been telling him to keep out of trouble, prevent embarrassment, accept that there was a division – a professional division – between subversion and crime. He looked down into Lavinia Dawson's face and saw huge, dark eyes, flecked with white and somehow, in his misery and isolation, saw – perhaps he imagined it – a flicker of alliance.

'Of course I'll go,' he said, quietly.

'Col . . .' said Tommy.

Sedately Cheyney took Tommy's left arm and, at Lavinia Dawson's direction, retraced his steps towards Birdcage Walk. Their escort came neatly, silently, and efficiently up behind them. They found a Jaguar saloon car illegally parked on the green side of Cockpit Steps, a grey-uniformed chauffeur holding open the rear door. That man and Cheyney came briefly into contact and Cheyney's gun was neatly taken away from him. Then Cheyney was in the back seat of the car, with a bodyguard on either side of him. Lavinia Dawson and Tommy were huddled in the front beside the driver. She leant over to him, and said: 'Hold out your arm, please, Colonel Cheyney,' and he did so, meekly.

The drug, Cheyney afterwards knew, was some mild hallucinogenic, but with soporific qualities. He had lost any real consciousness before they had gone a hundred yards, and the succeeding hours were a long series of vistas of nightmares. Faces and memories swam before his eyes and his mind, visions of disruption and terror and distraction. All the grosser sexual fantasies he went through. Colours deeper than ever they were in nature burned into his eyeballs. He had only the vaguest understanding of distance being covered, a place being reached, bars being locked about him while he was screaming, and a long, slow haul back to contact with other human beings, the end of which found him, his clothes torn and mired, sitting in a huge wooden chair in a gigantic room facing the fattest man he had ever seen.

He licked his dry lips with a dry tongue and said, 'What time is it?'

'Midnight, Mr Cheyney,' said Quex, with a deep and throaty chuckle. 'Midnight. You have been through my softening process. What do you remember? The beatings? The bars? A cage, I assure you, does indeed a prison make. And your cage, my dear Colonel, is now my will. However, there is whisky at your right hand.'

There was. Cheyney lapped greedily and recovered himself, then began to sip. There were cigarettes, too, and a lighter. Under the eye of the fat man Cheyney, whose hands, he saw with disgust, were shaking, lit a cigarette. He was barely focusing, and he was completely dominated by Quex.

That huge man sat behind an enormous desk. He was at least twenty-five stone, and seemed barely able to move. On his right, very close to the edge of the desk, sat Tommy, twitching, dribbling, trying to speak. On his left was Lavinia Dawson, wearing a long green dress, passive. The room was less a room than a hall. Its floor was tiled, not carpeted, and its roof was glass. It was oppressively heated, and around the walls – one of which was plate glass – was ranged an exotic collection of plants, tendrils curling up and down, spikes standing out, putrid life, rampant and devouring. They were, Cheyney's dull mind realised, in a conservatory, the centre part of which had been set out as an interview room. Behind his chair were two guards, subfusc, blandly dressed; behind Quex another; at the door two more. Each one was faceless, rigid, efficient, an automaton.

But Quex was himself his own prize exhibit. Cheyney's chair was on a much lower level than Quex's desk, so that his own eyes were on a level with its surface: Tommy and Lavinia Dawson were on the higher reach. From Quex's gigantic arms extruded two tiny, delicate hands, the hands of a fourteen-year-old; and one of them played constantly with a riding crop. The man was albino, but the apparently blind, light-sensitive eyes were not protected by glasses. The lushly pink skin poured sweat out and down into the purple suit, the even more purple shirt, until it dropped on the leather desk itself, forming a little pool in which Quex's left hand paddled.

'Look, Colonel Cheyney,' said Quex, 'at your fate.' He pointed to Tommy, and spoke in an easy, conversational, soft voice. 'I haven't put him on to hard drugs yet. I was just about to when I heard his father had been to see you, and I thought that you ought to see the decisive spectacle in the destruction of a boy before the man – you – was destroyed. We have been giving him six hundred milligrams of Chlorpromazine a day – by injection, actually, that is more convenient. I think I may start you on a thousand; your resistance is bound to be higher, and I look forward to a long and enjoyable period of breaking you.' He beamed and sweated and grunted. Tommy shifted. Like lightning the crop was in Quex's hand and Tommy had been cracked across the knuckles. He cried in pain, cried real tears, and sucked his hand. 'It is a wonderful drug,' said Quex meditatively.

'Why,' croaked Cheyney, 'why Tommy?'

'Goodness me,' said Quex, grinning and sweating. 'The woman, you fool. That crass fool Grey – useful, I freely admit, but wholly without a mind – indulged her, and she thought I would do the same. Stand up, Dawson.'

The woman rose. She had a full smile, and Cheyney saw that her eye teeth were more than ordinarily prominent. She turned slowly – pirouetted, almost – and showed that the back of her long green dress was cut almost to the buttocks. Her own back was marked with terrible weals.

'I did it myself,' said Quex, not without pride. 'I did it when she conceived what she, in her vulgar way, calls a fancy for this pup. So I thought I would bring him along as well, to show her. He was half-touched – she had seen to that. And I now have him to play with.'

'And you had Grey killed?' said Cheyney.

He could not have expected a better result. The woman, in the middle of her return pirouette, froze, and screamed.

'Clemmie,' she screamed and 'Clemmie,' she crooned. 'Is Clemmie gone too?'

But before the tableau of horror and emotion could freeze Quex interrupted roughly and good-humouredly. His hand had made only a twitch towards the riding crop. Then he said: 'Of course, my dear, of course.'

'Now' – this to the man behind him – 'take Lavinia and the boy away. Colonel Cheyney and I must talk.'

'Drugs,' said Quex, in his conversational tone, as Tommy and Lavinia were taken away. 'Drugs,' and he shook his head almost sadly.

'And now,' he said, shifting back to Cheyney with the eager and hospitable air of a man putting himself wholly at the disposal of a valued guest. 'I expect, Mr Cheyney, that there are things you want to ask me.' He nodded to Cheyney's right. 'There is more whisky there, good whisky. Drink deeply, my dear man, for it is the last alcohol you will ever touch.'

'I have noticed,' he added as an afterthought, 'that folk who take drugs lose interest in alcohol. And you will, of course, be on – I believe that is the word – drugs for the rest of your life. I must say, I have never touched either myself.'

Cheyney's body was entirely flaccid, and it was merely an academic exercise to calculate angles and distances and realise that, even fit, he had no chance of getting past Quex and the three silent sentries. Whatever drugs he had so far been fed, however, they had not yet killed his interest in whisky. He poured and drank, and asked Quex the question he always first asked himself:

'Where are we?'

Quex's chuckle rose from his belly, rumbled in his chest and reached his throat only at the last possible moment. 'Beguile yourself not with ideas of escape,' he said. 'But I do not mind answering your question. We are near a village in Surrey called South Holmwood. I am the happy and rich possessor of this large and beautiful house, which is surrounded by National Trust woods. It is understood that I am a scientist of large means, and my privacy is, naturally, respected.'

He waited, in complete peace. With his right hand Cheyney felt his collar, and realised that it had been ripped – by himself, presumably. He inspected himself. His clothes were torn, dirty, filthy with vomit. His hands – dirty themselves, he noticed with horror, the fingernails blackened – shook, as he put glass or cigarette to his mouth. Only that morning he had been defiant. Now, just one tiny, independent part of his brain was functioning, identifying and photographing this gross Buddha of an enemy sitting above him. For the rest of him, he fed it with whisky and nicotine and it took up nourishment like a traveller in the desert. He said, in his croak:

'What are you?'

'Ah.' Mr Quex was delighted. 'I am a man with twenty million pounds and a hobby, that of destruction. Naturally, since I love my native land, I want it to be the first beneficiary of my hobby. I am the largest importer of drugs into Britain, Mr Cheyney, and I let them go at giveaway prices. I subsidise innumerable causes, and innumerable people whom you would, in your vulgar way, call subversive. Even my fortune, of course, is not large enough, given present returns on investment, to pay for all of that, so I subvent my income with that of others, owning a plenitude of money, who share my aims, if not my fun.'

'Mad,' said Cheyney, as much to himself as to Quex.

'Oh, Mr Cheyney,' said Quex, pumping out air through his fat lips. 'You are behind the times. Have you ever seen a magazine called *Case Con*?' He waved something in front of Cheyney's bleared eyes. 'I quote from an admirable thinker, who has much influenced me, whose name is Mr Conduit.'

And quote he did, sonorously, carefully. 'Mental disorder,' he intoned, 'is false consciousness. Everybody is oppressed by the capitalist system, but some people are not aware of the social causes and are thus screwed up. The way out is to accept a Marxist analysis, whereupon they could cease to be mentally ill.'

'You are no Communist.'

'Of course not.' Quex was shocked. 'But I find what they have to say immensely comforting. Take, for example, that lovely phrase, "screwed up". It has a sexual connotation. I am, as you may have guessed, incapable of fornication. I am, indeed, incapable of most things that you value. I cannot consume alcohol without being sick, and I take no delight in what you call art. But I am happy in an ability to make money, and in finding other people who share my taste for disorder. In three weeks, Mr Cheyney, I shall have brought into this country, in one shipment, the means

125

of pleasure for an entire generation, and a man to organise its distribution.'

There was a long, long silence. Quex became impatient, almost worried.

'Come, come, Mr Cheyney,' he said, rumbling and coughing. 'You would not deny an old albino millionaire his little bit of pleasure? The amount of time I allow for debate is very limited. Tomorrow you will have a thousand milligrams of Chlorpromazine for breakfast, and I will not want to talk to you thereafter, only look at you.'

Cheyney had often faced the theory of anarchy; he had even fought some of its representatives. But he was intellectually, as well as physically, lost in his confrontation with Quex. Cheyney had imagination, but it was of a necessarily limited kind. When he had seen, expressed in action, the ideal of destruction for its own sake, he had assumed it to be the prerogative of the youthful or half-witted: either class could, in his view, be whipped into shape pretty quickly – mainly by being asked or required to face up to some personal difficulty. He had, of course, seen how clever men, whether urged on by political ideas or by the urge to profit, had exploited the self-indulgent, the kind of youthful wreck he had seen around Piccadilly. He had never before faced a man with power who, disinterestedly, wanted to destroy.

Quex sensed his confusion.

'It is my whim, Mr Cheyney,' he said with great gentleness. 'It is my whim. It is difficult to understand, is it not?'

What Cheyney could not understand was the simple proposition of Quex. He could not grasp the fact that a man so wholly unprepossessing, so bereft of charm or physical capacity, could have fought his way to financial power without acquiring any of the conformist ambitions which drew self-made millionaires into Cheyney's ken. Yet, it was so.

Even then, Cheyney thought, Quex could not live by himself. And so he framed another question:

'Who are you bringing in?'

'An intelligent question, Mr Cheyney, an intelligent question. An old adversary, as it happens, of your own, one Anatol Vishinsky. It was his boy, incidentally, who gave that glorious cry and killed the tiresome Grey the other evening.'

And killed Nelson, said a voice in Cheyney's head, and killed Nelson. 'Why do you need him?' he asked.

The piggish little eyes looked out of the huge sweaty face and Quex produced his *coup de grâce*. 'Because, Mr Cheyney, in a year, perhaps two, I will be dead, and my work must be carried on by strong young hands. Vishinsky, my dear man, is my heir!'

'He killed Richmond,' Cheyney muttered, rambling.

'Indeed he did.' Mr Quex was happy again, applauding a bright pupil. 'Indeed he did. You *are* intelligent on your last night among the sane, Mr Cheyney.'

But poor Cheyney's brain was in fragments. Quex was mad, Quex was powerful, Quex's activity was destruction, Quex's allies were people whose ideology was destruction, Quex was dying, Vishinsky was taking over and, as Colonel Cheyney slid down to destruction, his greatest rival would arrive to establish himself in wealth, power and security in Britain. His hand slipped as he reached for his glass.

'You are tired, Mr Cheyney,' said Quex, sorrowfully. 'You will find that, unlike the late Mr Grey, I keep a genuinely safe house. I am sorry this conversation could not have been a longer one. But no doubt dear Anatol will want words with whatever is left of you in three weeks' time.'

A last spasm of activity came to Cheyney. He rose screaming from his chair and lurched, hands, claws, outstretched for the bloated figure ahead of him. Quex was hydra-headed, and Cheyney grabbed in turn at each of the huge faces that drifted in at him, mocking his attempts to kill, his futile sentences of death. Then he fell over the step going up to Quex's desk and was carried away.

CHAPTER FIFTEEN

Loch Hill

Cheyney awoke. None of his possessions had been taken away from him, and he saw from his watch that it was three in the morning. A faint, almost a dying lamp burned high in the ceiling above him and, with its help, he looked around.

It was indeed a more straightforwardly secure prison than any Clement Grey had ever devised. Cheyney was in a barred cage, one, he quickly saw, of several. There were bars on three sides and a wall on the fourth: it was dank, and Cheyney supposed that he was underground. The cage on the left of his pallet was empty, but there was somebody on his right. Still groggy, Cheyney made his way across the cement floor and looked down on a sleeping, sweaty, twitching, Tommy Graham.

But Cheyney was now drained, of anger, of hate, of fear. There was an exhausted flicker of disgust when he looked again at his clothes. Tommy stank. The boy was obviously wearing whatever he had on when he had left – had been taken from – his parents' house all that time ago. He had never washed or changed since then. Of this Cheyney became aware at the same time as he realised what had brought him awake – the driving need to piss. And then he saw that Tommy's pallet was stained and surrounded by excrement. Hubert Quex did not completely rely on drugs.

In the worst and most incomprehensible trouble he had ever been in, Cheyney, minded to throw himself back on his miserable bed and almost cry his way to sleep, recalled a maxim handed down to him twenty-five years ago by the man who had trained him, Peter Hannay. 'When you are in the worst fix,' Hannay had said, 'take the offensive. Take it for yourself, not for what damage it may cause the enemy.' Cheyney remembered Hannay's words as though they were issuing from that lean, dedicated face at just that moment. 'Take the offensive for yourself,' he muttered.

He went to the bars of his cage and pissed into the corridor. He came back to the bed and took off all his clothes. With hard exercise – fifty push-ups and fifty sit-ups – he tried to shake himself back into reasonable shape. He tore the tail off his shirt and used it to dry-scrub his vomit-ridden trousers. Then, light-headed but clear, he put his ruined clothes on again, lay down on the bed and lit the second last of his cigarettes. Though he could see no hope, his humour was restored, and he drifted into sleep thinking that nicotine was not a particularly good *apéritif* for a breakfast of Chlorpromazine.

But the dreams came; and the faces. They swam and eddied about him and brought him horror. The dominant, and still crude, face was that of Lavinia Dawson, screaming and crying that something had been done to Clemmie. Strange, Cheyney thought in his restless sleep, that the criminal classes had a sense of kin similar to the rest of us. He turned on his pallet and was suddenly and completely awake, for the stricken face next to his own was – it was *not* a dream – Lavinia Dawson's. Gently, carefully, he rose on his hip and began to stroke her hair: it was coarse, that raven effect an illusion. 'Yes,' he said soothingly, 'Quex had Clemmie killed.'

He paused, and took another risk. 'And you owe Clemmie.'

She was lying on the bed, eyes almost vacant, her back,

his exploring left hand told him, still wounded, sore, stiff and ribbed from Quex's mad punishment. But his cage was open.

'He was nice, Clemmie,' she said. She was clearly drugged, her flecked eyes staring and finding it difficult to focus. She represented for Cheyney a chance that would never come again.

'Lavinia,' he said very carefully, using her name for the first time. 'I was with Grey when he was killed.'

She pulled her head back from him and tried again to focus on his face. He spoke softly, urgently. 'You must help me to get Tommy out of here. Is his cage open?'

She shook her head, incapable of consecutive thought.

'I'm with Mr Quex,' she said finally.

'How many others are there in the house?' He forced himself to combine the urgency necessary to keep her awake and thinking with the calmness needed to avoid frightening her. He was sorely tempted to stun her and try to fight his own way out, but her action in coming down to him, raddled as she was, gave some hope that she might provide invaluable help. Cheyney suddenly realised that he was sweating with nerves.

He eased himself and the woman slowly into sitting positions. Then he started to stand up. She grabbed his arm and started to cry. For God's sake, she was going to scream.

He put a hand firmly and gently over her face. 'I must get Tommy out,' he said simply, 'you see that, don't you? Otherwise they'll kill him the way they killed Clemmie. You don't want that, do you?'

Dumbly, under his hand, she shook her head.

'You can come with us,' said Cheyney, dividing his attention between her and his surroundings, trying to plan ahead, conscious even then of the stink and the barbarity, desperate to be away and out into the night. What, he wondered, would Simon Collins think of all this activity on the part of a middle-aged Civil Servant?

She shook her head again, made a great effort to speak and said, with great finality, 'I stay. I'm with Mr Quex now.'

'Then you must get back to your room. If he finds you here he'll beat you again.'

She shuddered away in horror: whatever masochism had been in her before, whatever foul impulse had attracted her to Quex, it had gone now. In her fear she gained strength, and stood up, quickly and fluently.

'Is there a guard?' Cheyney had to have this question answered, and she appeared co-operative.

'No. Lift. To ground floor.'

He did not believe her.

'Up.' She pointed an unsteady ringed finger at the ceiling. Then, as he turned her around, Cheyney saw a bunch of keys hanging from the lock of his own cage. Quex had to be confident, he thought, but he would have no reason to suspect the kind of mindless treason of which he was now the victim. 'How many,' asked Cheyney again, 'how many in the house?'

She frowned with the effort to concentrate, began to count on her fingers, swayed away so that he had to catch her and then, with a pleased smile, said, 'Ten.'

No good, then: hopeless, in fact. 'Where,' he said, with that quiet insistence, 'where does Quex keep his records – papers, things like that. Where?'

She flared. 'I'm not telling you. I'm with Mr Quex now.' She began to cry again, and mutter to herself that Grey was dead.

Cheyney dared not wait. While she was sniffling he got her over to the gate of his own cage, and then a step down the corridor, keys in hand, to Tommy's. Still supporting Lavinia, he got that open, sweating with relief, lowered her to the floor where she now sat giggling and shook the boy awake.

Relief flooded through him as Tommy sat up. The boy was still sweating and twitching, but there was intelligence in his eyes. Cheyney spoke very quickly:

'Tommy, I'm getting you out of here right away. How fit are you?'

'Oh God,' said Tommy, 'Uncle Allen.' And he too burst into tears.

Cheyney forced himself to wait for the storm to subside, though he was growing increasingly desperate, and beginning to wonder how much time he had. His mind was near to snapping point, with the boy shaking uncontrollably on his shoulder and Lavinia Dawson alternating between giggles and tears behind him. At last Tommy was quiet.

'Now Tommy, three things you must tell me, quickly. Do you know the way out? Where is the garage? And where does Quex keep papers – you know, files, records, that sort of thing?'

Tommy made a heroic effort to concentrate, and he succeeded, but when he spoke his voice was slow and the words were punctuated by gasps. 'Up,' he managed, 'one floor in the lift. The greenroom is there. Only papers I saw in the desk. Door near greenroom to the garden.' And that seemed as much as he could manage.

Colonel Cheyney did not have the strength to carry both of them. He got Tommy to his feet and slung him over one shoulder. Then out into the corridor, risking a left turning and, in a moment, there was the blessed lift, its call button staring unblinkingly at the bars of another cage. 'Can you stand?' Cheyney whispered, and when Tommy nodded vigorously he left him leaning against the lift and went back for Lavinia. She had passed out, exhausted by the efforts she had made.

Cheyney was himself near collapse. The recovery that

his violent exercise had induced was only temporary: whatever drug he had been given was having its effect again, and the desperate nervous tension he now suffered almost unmanned him. And there was no sign of a weapon, or anything that could be used as one, anywhere.

He manhandled Lavinia to the lift, muttered a prayer, and pressed the button. Seconds later he was standing, with Tommy beside him, in a spacious tiled hall, lit by a faint night light. The girl was slumped in his arms, and he was facing the doors to the greenroom. He now saw that the hall and the exit were at one extreme end of the house and that the greenroom had been built as an extension to the main building. 'What's there?' he asked Tommy, pointing to a door on the other side of the hall.

Tommy looked at it vacantly. 'Room,' he said finally.

'It'll have to do,' muttered Cheyney. He staggered towards it with his burden, opened the door and, in the darkness, got Lavinia into a chair.

And then he realised his mistake; and how he had been semi-consciously lied to.

As he came out of the room, into the spacious hall, exhausted and only half-thinking he heard the steady and bored pace of the armed guard who was coming from the kitchen under the stairs and advancing towards him. At the same moment they saw one another.

And then Cheyney collapsed.

He – or his shallow, sweaty, shabby figure – fell directly at the feet of a man on the most tedious duty of all – protecting a place believed by all who inhabited it to be beyond attack. Any guard work is dull. The man required to guard something, or some place, that is safe as well becomes unsafe.

More. The sound of Cheyney had convinced the man who came from the kitchen that he had been detected in a minor crime, stealing from the larder.

As he hesitated, Cheyney was gathering his last strength. Here was a large and strong young man, clothed in some uniform, carrying a gun. There a man in middle age, already abusing his last resources.

But Cheyney recalled Pierce's effort; swore not to be outdone; took the guard's ankle; swung him against the wall; and smashed the butt of the man's own pistol again and again into his head until he paused in an action of destruction more disgusting than his own initial fear.

But it could not all have taken more than a few seconds. He ran his left hand across his forehead, and realised that he should take this opportunity of acquiring a weapon. The gun had come free. On his knees now Cheyney reached out for it, steadying himself against the body of his victim. His hand touched a heavy leather belt and, then, oddly, a sheath.

The dully surviving spark of curiosity in his brain saved him. He had drawn out the knife and was looking at it in a puzzled fashion when he heard the movement from behind.

From Quex's room came the second guard. As Cheyney came round, still on his knees, the man's gun was coming up in his right hand and his left was bringing a whistle to his mouth.

Cheyney was on his right knee, his right buttock resting on his heel and his foot folded into the floor. The knife was in his left hand.

He came off the floor like a recoiling spring. His arms stretched out ahead of him. He left the ground in his leap, and the knife went into the guard, right up to the haft.

For more seconds – it seemed hours – Cheyney lay half sprawled across his victim's body. He did not move; Tommy did not move; nothing seemed to move. Had another guard been posted Cheyney would have been finished. There was no other. He got to his feet.

'The garage, Tommy,' he found himself whispering furiously, his fingers cutting into the boy's arm, 'where's the garage?'

Tommy pointed at the front door.

'Sit down,' Cheyney told him. Tommy sat on one of the hall chairs and Cheyney waited for a few seconds, gathering strength and listening furiously to the almost inaudible night murmurs of a large and silent house.

Then he was off again, flitting across the hall and into the greenroom, silent, ghostly, a preposterous place with its huge dais and massive desk. In a sliver of moonlight he found his way to the desk and, intense though his concentration was, felt renewed surprise at the girth of the desk chair, presumably specially built to accommodate Quex. He chanced the desk light, but the drawers were locked.

Everything had to be risked now. A heavy steel paper knife got him into the drawers. He was very nearly in a panic, his nerves taut to the point of breaking, his fear growing with every second, that he would be re-taken with, this time, no chance of escape. He took all the papers he could find – there was a surprising quantity – and raced back into the hall, pushing them into the hands of an uncomprehending Tommy. Then he was back in the greenroom, dragging covers from chairs and piling them into the knee-holes of the desk. Then, back in the hall again and carefully – oh, so carefully – letting Tommy and himself out into the night.

By the moonlight Cheyney could see that the garage was, in fact, a modern, flimsily constructed shed of large proportions. It was, by the mercy of God, unlocked. Inside there were four large cars, and space for more. Carefully Cheyney fumbled his way along one of the walls and, at the very back of the shed, found two areas walled off from the rest of the storage space. One was a workroom, and

Cheyney thankfully exchanged his paper knife for a healthy spanner. Here, too, he found a torch, and risked a quick flash. No amount of gold could have, for him, exceeded the riches he found.

On pegs above the worktable were neatly hung the keys of the cars, the registration number of each carefully recorded on cards below. In the storage space on the other side of the shed, Cheyney found what he had been praying for, but had not hoped to find, a petrol pump.

Moments later he had filled a large jerry can. Then he went back to Tommy carrying it, the torch and all the car keys. There was no business of selection, he picked the car nearest the door – a year-old model – and got Tommy and his precious cargo unceremoniously bundled into it. Carrying the petrol can, Cheyney went back to the house, through the main door, and into the greenroom.

It took him some moments to prepare a pyre. Chair covers and rugs came first. Then curtains were yanked from their hangings, each layer of material laced with petrol. The blotting paper from the desk was taken, and newspapers and magazines found in a corner of the room added sheet by sheet to his pile, every combustible sheet soaked and soaked again until there was nothing left in Cheyney's can.

As he looked at the soggy mess he wished he had had paraffin, the effect of which he knew. Finally, he lit a torch of newspaper and threw it at his pile.

There was a pause, and a whoosh, and a flame burned its way across – as it seemed – his whole face. He reeled back, breath and sight temporarily gone, and reached the door behind him. He made his way to the front and paused a moment to breathe in the suddenly sweet and reviving night air.

Then he was off in a shambling run to the car.

CHAPTER SIXTEEN

Preparations

Cheyney made the run from Surrey to Carlisle in six frantic hours. An hour and a half later he was sitting in the living room of a friend, Malcolm Ross, with whom he regularly climbed. In Ross's surgery Tommy was sleeping.

Ross poured more coffee for Cheyney – clean and content for the first time in what seemed weeks, dressed in his friend's old clothes and remembering a splendid breakfast.

'I've given the lad some Kemadrin,' said Ross, an angular, humorous, lithe man, with a shock of very fair hair and a notable coolness in coping with an old friend who arrives in tatters and in the company of a drugged boy in a stolen car at breakfast-time. The car was now safely under cover in Ross's garage, Cheyney's and Tommy's clothes were on the doctor's bonfire. Already Cheyney's mind was moving to Loch Hill as Ross continued his explanation:

'Essentially the drug they used induces effects somewhat like those of Parkinson's disease, so the quickest remedy is an anti-Parkinson drug – and I prefer Kemadrin. I've given him ten mils and that should take away most of the stiffness and the twitching you noticed.'

'Is there likely to be any permanent effect? He's been on this other drug for quite some time.'

Ross shook his head. 'Shouldn't think so. You're on to Loch Hill? Well, a few days there will do him good. Chlorpromazine shouldn't have any addictive effect on a youngster with his basic good health, but you'll find him a bit fey for a few days, I shouldn't wonder. I've made up some tablets for him, and I'll run over in a while to look at him.'

Ross began to fill a pipe. 'Now, Allen, can I for God's sake have the story.'

'Sorry, Malcolm,' Cheyney stood up. 'I must be on my way. If you fancy a tramp in a couple of weeks you can have the lot. The job's not over yet. Can I use your phone?'

'You were always the same,' said Ross, not ungraciously, and he left Cheyney to telephone a delirious Peter Graham.

On the drive from Carlisle to Loch Hill, Tommy, sitting beside Cheyney in the front seat, was nervous and silent. After a stammering attempt at thanks he had scarcely spoken that morning. With this state of affairs Cheyney was well content. He preferred to leave it to Peter Graham to bring the boy back to life, and he had already worked out to his own satisfaction the answers to most of the questions which, a few days ago, he would have been desperate to ask Tommy. Besides, he had great hopes of the treasure trove he had taken from Quex's house: the fire, he trusted, would have concealed his activities and he reckoned that Quex – somehow he couldn't believe that he had perished in the conflagration – would long have left Surrey – unnecessarily, since Cheyney had now decided to play his own game, and – risk-taking as ever – had no intention of bringing the police into the action.

Loch Hill stands on a craggy rise at the head of a small glen. It overlooks, as its name would convey, a small reed-ridden loch, surrounded on the far side by hawthorn, which effectively shields the house from the road. On the right is the small damson orchard and rose garden, which Cheyney had found neglected and overgrown and had carefully restored: on the left, rock, fern and gorse provide a protection. Although the sixteenth-century house cannot be viewed by travellers on the road, as soon as a car enters the glen on the Dumfries side, it can be seen from Loch Hill.

As always, at the entrance to the glen Cheyney stopped and lit a cigarette, gazing through the chill autumn day up the rise to where his beloved house nestled behind its screen. No Nelson, this time, he thought, though he could rely for service on the Burnses, husband and wife, who lived nearby in what had once been the local primary school, and who looked after Loch Hill in his absence.

Tommy stirred and got out of the car. He was now clean and dressed in jeans and a sweater belonging to Malcolm Ross's son. The wind, as it whipped towards them down the glen, tossed his hair across his face and he brought a hand over to shield his eyes. There was a flush and almost a sparkle to them.

Then he looked shyly across at Cheyney. 'Do you have the whole glen?'

'Yes. I rent out most of the farming land, of course.' He grinned like a boy. 'When I retire, I'll take some of it back and put my roots down in heather.'

Then, in an easy and companionable way, and as though the dreadful last weeks had not existed, they got back into the car and drove on to the house.

The car had, of course, been seen, and three figures waited for them. Peter Graham tore down from the house, the seamed worry, anxiety and hostility wholly vanished from his big, open face, and threw his arms round the boy. Over Tommy's shoulder Cheyney could see that he was crying and, as their eyes met, Cheyney was powerfully aware of his old friend's mute gratitude. His voice unsteady, Peter said: 'I've told Maria. But' – this with some puzzlement even through his joy – 'I've told her not to come up. She says she understands.'

Emotion made Cheyney uncomfortable and he nodded

and said crisply. 'Good. Tommy'll be fine. Take him for a stroll now, there's a good chap, and we'll lunch in half an hour.'

Then he turned his back to smile at the intensely mundane Burns, who was eyeing the Jaguar doubtfully. 'It's not mine,' said Cheyney, cheerfully, 'I've stolen it, but we'll hang on to it for a few more days.' Cheyney went inside to change with more cheer of heart than he had known for many weeks.

After lunch, and before a roaring fire, Colonel Cheyney held his first council of war. Despite – or perhaps because of – the Kemadrin, Tommy had seemed exhausted and, after they had eaten, he had gone to bed. Briefly Graham learned from Cheyney that what he had expected was true: Tommy had formed one of those inexplicable attachments to the stripper he had in all fun hired for his ball: she had returned the attraction, if not the affection, and he had been led into her strange life, taking the badge from her flat as a memento. When he had decamped from his parents' house to go to Lavinia, he had left it behind.

'Don't think too badly of her,' Cheyney said to Graham at the end of the recital, 'mad and evil as she may be, we would not be here if it wasn't for her.' And with that the subject was forever closed with them.

Cheyney got up to charge their glasses before briefing Graham – who evidently had not grasped that, with Tommy back, the affair was still far from closed – when Mrs Burns came into the room. 'Sir,' she said, 'there's a car turning into our road end.'

Cheyney put down the glass and decanter he had been holding, went to the window and picked up his glasses. A blue Capri was negotiating the rutted road to the house. Graham was beside Cheyney, sensing his tension. 'What is it?' he asked tightly.

'By God,' said Cheyney, more to himself than Graham,

'The Musketeers are assembling.' Then he put down his glasses and went out to greet Chief Superintendent Pierce.

Once given a whisky Pierce explained himself with a brevity so marked that in any other man it would have been impossibly artificial.

'I got the same kind of row from my bosses as you, I believe, did from yours. The suggestion was made, none too kindly, that I was devoting too much manpower to the whole business, and especially to the question of young Tommy. It was put to me that I was under strain and I agreed to take a month's leave. I heard about your man and what had happened to you. I reckoned I'd find you here.'

Cheyney recounted his own adventures, and Pierce and Graham listened intently. At the conclusion the policeman said, 'But what the hell are you playing at?'

'I want Vishinsky,' Cheyney said simply. 'I don't want him arrested, or imprisoned, or exchanged. I'm going to kill him.' He paused and drank some whisky. 'And after that I'm going to kill Quex.'

'No,' said Peter Graham with finality, 'Quex is mine.'

Cheyney looked at him. 'I asked you up here because you would want to be in at the end of the hunt,' he said.

For a long time Pierce gazed into the heart of the fire. His face was less impassive, and they could see the struggle on it. He was a policeman, and professionally what they were proposing was inexcusable. But Cheyney had not mistaken his man. Finally, Pierce looked up. 'I won't stand in your way,' he said, 'but what have you got?'

For answer Cheyney brought him the papers taken from the greenroom. 'They're not properly sorted or read yet,' he explained, 'but I had a quick whistle through them this morning, while a friend was looking after Tommy. I'll go through them properly when we've finished talking, and you, Pierce, can have them after dinner. But the main thing we've got here, partly in note form and partly in code, is a skeleton picture of Quex's operations in Britain.'

The eternal gleam of the hunter was in Pierce's eyes.

'Jesus,' he said, reverently.

Cheyney nodded briskly. 'Now, there's also a diary,' he said, producing a thick, loose-leaf book. 'Some of the entries are incomprehensible, all are in abbreviated form. But I want you to take a look. See here, "V to come." "Contact with V." "M gone to V." "V coming." And look at this, "V's date, Solway."'

'He's coming up the Firth?' asked Graham, incredulously.

'I doubt if it's up the Firth. Probably not right up, but to one of the small inlets. I have an idea or two where it might be, and tomorrow I'll scout around a few chums and see what's what. By my reckoning they must have a house round here, some sort of base, and it's very unusual for Midlanders or Londoners – who make up most of our residential visitors – to be in residence at this time of year. Once we know what we're looking for it won't be difficult to spot.'

He wrapped his fingers round his glass and leaned forward to look into the fire. His eyes were blazing.

'You know how it is,' he said, 'when bits and pieces have been around in your head for a long time and then suddenly they come together? We have a few facts. Quex is a manic destroyer, a madman, impotent and apparently dying. He's using a large fortune to help on destruction, and he's tied in with the Russians. Vishinsky is coming over as, you might say, managing director, and chairman designate.'

'But,' Pierce objected, 'Vishinsky could come to Britain in the normal way, surely, even as a diplomat.'

Cheyney shook his head. 'No. He is one of the very few that even this government wouldn't have here at any price. Half the defence staff would resign if he were allowed entry.

But underground he could do a terrific job, and if our experience and these papers are anything to go by, Quex's organisation can easily support him. Anyway let me go on.

'The other facts we have are these. Quex is into drugs and espionage in a big way; probably into straightforward crime as well, though we can't be sure. He is expecting – he told me this – the biggest drug shipment this country has ever seen and Vishinsky with it. My bet is that it's coming here, to this side of the Firth where there are more secluded coves. It can't be just a simple landing, they must have a base and a support staff in situ. I reckon we take them as they land. Remember this is old smuggling country, and with coastguarding in the way it is today, a well-financed organisation would have no trouble.'

'But Cheyney,' said Pierce, 'won't your activities in Surrey put them off? Surely Quex will suspect what you've found out and lie low for a bit?'

'You haven't met him. He has the most colossal ego, and he's quite insane in the degree of his self-esteem. None the less, he has a kind of empathy: he could understand that I would do something like that in sheer horror at his existence.'

Cheyney seemed restless, and took a turn around the room. Then he turned again and faced them.

'I spend hours every day just reading papers. All sorts of papers. Papers from you, Pierce, papers from all over Whitehall. I spend most of my time looking for connections. And I live here. It's been comment for months that the old smuggling trade is reviving in this part of the world. It's a common belief – a professional belief – that we're getting control of it, especially drugs, elsewhere. Don't you both see? They've been opening up a new route here. But what's the point if the shipments are continuing to be as compact as they've always been? The big ports are the right places for everything we've known up to now. So *this* is where they're coming.'

His eyes were blazing with their pale fire again. Then they went quiet and he made a little gesture with his right hand. 'It's a gamble,' he said, 'but I'm right.'

Pierce rubbed his chin: 'It's chancy; and how do we find Quex after this mysterious landing of yours?'

Cheyney held up a simple black address book. 'I found this in his desk. It's lettered from A to M and there are varying numbers of addresses under each letter. My reading of the situation is that these addresses are in descending order of importance, and that the A's are Quex's own safe houses. There are only four of them and the Surrey house is first.'

'Good,' said Pierce, 'but not, to be honest, completely convincing.'

'It'll do for a start.' Cheyney knew deep down that he was right in what he had deduced, every bone in his body told him.

'Well,' said Pierce, 'I said I'd go along with you and I will, but I'm breaking every rule in the book. Can we go through those papers before dinner? I'm impatient.'

'Of course, but that bit about rules worries me.'

'Don't worry. If Quex is as big as we've always thought he was – even when we didn't know who he was – and if those papers of yours are what you think they are, I'm in clover. Any misdemeanours will be forgotten and forgiven.'

'Anyway, you haven't heard what I'm planning to do yet.' And quietly, in detail, he explained his plan to them. When he had finished, Graham was the first to speak.

'I'm game,' he said, 'but it strikes me that you are going to be the one in danger of losing a job, Allen.'

'If so, it wouldn't really matter. But I doubt it. The local Chief Constable and the Procurator are both very close friends of mine and they'll swallow it in London if I get Vishinsky, dead or alive.'

'And where do I come into it?' asked Pierce.

'There's a pleasant little sailing village near here and I want you to go over there in a day or two. Let them believe you've driven up from London. Take a room in the Anchor Hotel. Then, just before *Der Tag*, I want you to get into conversation with the landlord; tell him you know me and that you have an idea that I have a place up here; telephone me and I'll invite you to stay. You will be due here on the day after the action. I'll speak to Dave Mackenzie and tell him that only a fraction of the stuff I've got is in his territory, and it's really your case. Then I'll give it to you – subject to one proviso, that I have a clear forty-eight hours on the "A" addresses.'

'Somebody's going to have to swallow a hell of a lot of coincidence,' said Graham, dubiously.

'They'll swallow it. They'll swallow when they see fishes in our net.'

'When's the day?' asked Pierce.

'Eleven days from now, according to my calculations,' said Cheyney soberly. 'I've got eleven days to find their landing point and make my plans. Now, do you want to go through these files with me?'

'One thing before we do. Is this place safe? The address, if I remember rightly, is in *Who's Who?*'

Cheyney smiled. 'I'm not averse to Quex coming after us, if that's what you mean. I'd prefer him not to, prefer to save him for the end of the meal. So. He'll know, if his sources are anything like as good as I think they must be, that I'm in trouble, in disgrace, if you like. I've even arranged for a friend to raise my extraordinary behaviour in the House; and for it to get about that I've gone abroad with my brother. Though actually I think Quex will want to save me for later.'

146

He got up and went to the window.

'But from this evening we'll not be unprotected here. This is where I took Charlie Mason, and not a word reached the outside. You must have noticed the capacity of the glen for defence. And by tonight I'll have it under guard.'

He turned back to them.

'You can sleep soundly until Vishinsky comes.'

CHAPTER SEVENTEEN

Battle

It was a bitterly cold and starless night as, without lights, the broad-beamed old tramp steamer edged its way along the Galloway coast. Impervious, it seemed, even to a still cold that bit through the toughest and warmest clothing, a tall man in a leather jacket stood on the bridge beside the Captain and gazed unwaveringly at the little dots of yellow along the coast, signalling habitation, warmth, comfort, something out of this bleak, black seascape.

'When do you put us over?' asked the tall man, his tone suggesting indifference rather than interest. He buried his hands in his jacket pockets as he spoke.

'Twenty minutes about from now,' the Captain, who was Scottish, told him. 'Will ye find yer way?'

'I expect so. Are you nervous?'

'Of course I'm bloody nervous. Three men and those parcels. What kind of a mug d'ye think I am? It's drugs, that's what it is. Christ, I never seen so much stuff.' His voice had almost a touch of reverence.

'There's nothing for you to worry about,' Vishinsky assured him, turning his lean, bony face, with its exophthalmic pale-blue eyes directly on the other. 'You have a legitimate reason to be in the Firth. When we are lowered you can forget you ever saw us, and merely go ahead and pick up the rest of your fee.' His voice hardened. 'It has always seemed to me that it was, for what you are doing, an exceptionally generous one.'

Vishinsky had a way of speaking, an ice-cold tone of

command, that shrivelled most people he used it on, and it shrivelled the Captain. He relapsed into the moodiest of silences, and swept the mysterious coast ahead of him with his nightglasses, uselessly.

They were travelling on – supposedly – very exact compass bearings, and the tramp's brief was to put Vishinsky and his companions down within striking longboat distance of one of the Firth inlets, where there subsisted even through the winter, knocked about and stained though they became, a small group of beach bungalows.

Vishinsky spent another few minutes alongside the Captain. His long nose was pointed towards the coast like the nose of an eager dog, scenting out prey ahead. He would have preferred that his return to Britain took place in a grander fashion, but he was happy to be coming back, happy with his cargo, happy with the elaboration and wealth of the strange organisation which he was joining, the head of which seemed to puzzle even his bosses. He took his hands out of his pockets and rubbed them together so hard and fast that, for a moment, they became warm from the friction.

Strange, Vishinsky thought, how a coastline at night, at first though spotted with light, so apparently unchanging, remote, impenetrable, gained, after you had contemplated it for a time, a changing individuality of its own. He was becoming, he thought, attuned to travel by sea, might even begin to enjoy it. He listened to the soft splash of the water against the bows – at least it was a still night. He didn't fancy trying to make it across choppy water in a rowing boat. He shivered at the thought, and said to the Captain: 'I will make sure all is ready.'

The man nodded, and Vishinsky went slowly aft. There the two men who were to be his executive assistants and bodyguards were well clothed against the cold, sitting patiently by their boat. They were both tall – taller than he was himself – and, though deceptively slim in appearance, beautifully well-co-ordinated and well-muscled. Each spoke perfect English and had been thoroughly trained in the mores of the country where they would now spend at least the next three years, for the most part working under cover. He was lucky to have them, Vishinsky thought, but he could not repress a slight irritation at the fact that the subversion schools nowadays seemed to turn out semi-automatons. They had both risen at his approach and stood before him, respectfully, but not deferentially, waiting passively for instructions. He told them to check their loads again, and they bent to the task without a word.

He went himself to the rail and lit his last Russian cigarette. Now his mind turned out towards that dark, but blinking, coast, and he began to consider that part of his task which, until now, had been forced firmly into the back of his mind. He was once more in the field, and about to be the spearhead of what would, almost certainly, be the last necessary thrust against a tottering England. He always thought of the country like that, not as Great Britain, nor as the United Kingdom, but as England: he remembered Philby chiding him on the subject.

Vishinsky had always despised British tolerance, sneered at British democracy, laughed openly among his cronies at the country's increasing failure to defend itself – laughed as he carefully wove the web, out of strands from the IRA, from the crazy Hubert Quex – a bonus, that – out of strands from crime. But he had a queer, ineradicable regard for the place, a regard that was probably analogous to the regard conquerors have often had for the land they had subjugated. For some time, of course, Vishinsky realised, there would be no question of subjugating England: the object of the next five years was to weaken her as a friend to others, subvent everything in the country that was divisive and, above all, keep out of sight. Quex's criminal resources, Vishinsky realised, would, at the beginning at least, have to be used very sparingly indeed.

Then his thoughts, going out over the black water, moved to a face, just at the moment that the owner of that face was concentrating fiercely on him. It was unlikely, Vishinsky thought with regret, that he would come into direct contact with Colonel Cheyney, though he had been a trifle alarmed by a cryptic message from Quex mentioning the Colonel. Vishinsky had hoped to keep all knowledge of their activities from Cheyney for at least some considerable time yet. In the last battle between the two men it had been Vishinsky who was victorious but Cheyney, he was perfectly prepared to admit to himself, had a notch or two on his gun as well. And Cheyney on his home ground would be a good deal more formidable than Cheyney fighting on extended lines with inadequate means and uncertain allies in Eastern Europe. Still, there was no questioning his extraordinary flair, his ability to divine things when evidence was scrappy, disjointed, inadequate.

A voice behind him whispered, 'Ready now, sir.'

Vishinsky nodded and watched the boat being winched into position, his two young men prepared to take the oars. He scrambled aboard, and waved a hand back at the stinking tramp that had been his home now for ten days. Then he sank down in the stern sheets still in his reflective mood. The last message he had had radioed to him had told him of the killing of Grey and Nelson – messy that, but necessary – and the escape of Cheyney. Really, Vishinsky thought, the man's luck was extraordinary. But he genuinely regretted the death of Nelson. Cheyney's profile in his own file told a little of their long association and mutual devotion, and Vishinsky sincerely understood what he imagined would be Cheyney's distress.

Intelligence officers at the level of Cheyney and Vishinsky – whether they are subversives or counter-sub-versives – get to know one another rather as do people who play chess over radio at long distances. There need be no sympathy or similarity or personality – there was none whatever between Cheyney and Vishinsky – but their methods and working personalities became known to one another through what is attempted with, and what happens to, their chessmen, their agents. And there had been, fur-ther – what was very rare in their profession – a very high number of field contacts between the two men. They had both been in Korea, for example, and in Berlin. But what Vishinsky had most enjoyed in their long battle was his own time on the staff of the Russian Embassy in London. In retrospect, he was prepared to admit, it had been a mistake: the bravado inherent in his appointment had caused Cheyney and his Department to raise their en-deavours to mighty heights to have him thrown out, and when a Foreign Secretary at last listened to them, not only Vishinsky went, but many others as well. Still, Vishinsky thought contentedly, a new British government had re-versed all that, and his old colleagues were returning to London.

Ahead one brilliant lamp flared for a moment and was dead. One of the other men sighed. 'Almost there,' he said, speaking in English.

They were very close in now. One of the houses ahead of them was lighted, and from the pale gleams it threw out Vishinsky barely discerned a cluster of small buildings. Down at the very edge of the water the single light came to life again, and vanished. 'Fool,' thought Vishinsky, 'one alone was necessary.'

Then the boat hit the clay mud.

There was only one man waiting for them. In the very dim light the house threw out Vishinsky could see that he

152

was in tweeds, and wearing knickerbockers. He stood there casually, at ease, his left hand was behind his back, and over his right arm he carried a shotgun. At his feet Vishinsky could discern the bulk of his signalling lamp.

'Good evening,' he said.

'Fool,' hissed Vishinsky, 'you are using too much light.' His two men were hauling the boat up the strand. 'Where are my carriers?'

'Oh, I've got light enough,' said the tall man, 'light enough for you, my lad.'

A swathe of light cut through the dark and held the two men just long enough for Vishinsky to see his face.

'So,' he said with bile rising in his chest, up through his throat and into his mouth, 'Cheyney.'

Cheyney, the heavy shotgun still levelled, began to retreat. As he did the torchlight died and lamps came up. The new arrivals could see Graham, and Pierce and Burns, fanning back to keep them covered. They were helpless, and with their gestures they surrendered.

'Up to the house,' said Cheyney, stepping aside.

But as Vishinsky passed him Cheyney said to him, very softly, 'No, not you, my boy,' and the Russian stopped.

They waited until the others had gone by. Cheyney took a torch from his left-hand pocket and shone it full on Vishinsky. The shotgun he held one-handed but, awkward though the shooting posture was, Vishinsky would not have tried for the gun. Cheyney used the beam of the torch to indicate his wishes and Vishinsky turned to the left and walked ahead of him, parallel to the sea.

In a minute or two they were standing amid scrub on a small base of headland. The light of the torch dipped and the Russian saw, poised on a flat rock, a small wire cage. In it Cheyney placed the torch and at that moment the moon came through the clouds above them. There was almost light to shoot by, even without the torch. With his left hand Cheyney tossed cigarettes and matches on the ground by Vishinsky's feet.

'Bend slowly,' he said. 'But don't take a step.'

Vishinsky did so, and lit a cigarette. Cheyney gestured and the cigarettes and lighter were gently tossed back to his feet. A moment later, the gun crooked in his right arm, he too had lit a cigarette, and the two men might have been chatting quietly while awaiting a dawn flight of birds. The air about them was still and dry: there was a soft rustle in the scrub and through the sand at their feet and, nearby, the thump-thump of the waves and the occasional gentle splash.

Vishinsky's mouth was dry now, but with a rind of bile inside it.

'This is the end?' he asked simply.

'Yes. But I wanted you to know it.'

'Why? Nelson?'

'Yes.'

Vishinsky made a small gesture, and carefully tested the reflexes of his trembling knees.

'Men die every day in our service.' He managed a smile. 'You are setting a bad precedent. My people will come after you.'

'No. You will have died in action. You resisted, you see. You resisted arrest.'

Vishinsky turned slightly to look out to sea. They smoked on in an almost companionable silence. Vishinsky it was who seemed to want to speak. Cheyney's mind was now blank, and at peace.

The Russian flexed his legs again and turned.

Cheyney brought up his gun and fired.

Epilogue

'Only one more place to try, then,' said Graham as he dispiritedly studied the road map on his knees.

'We'll find him there,' said Cheyney.

Graham looked sideways at the friend who had done so much – and done so much for him – in the last few weeks. They were in the last few hours of the forty-eight allowed them, and so far they had drawn blank. Graham's mind went back to the long cold days of rest in Cheyney's house, his host out every day, all day, for a week, scouting his own native ground, stalking for enemies, for infiltrators, for raiders; and then returning one day, tired, excited, exhilarated, with his tale of an invading troop in a collection of beach bungalows.

God, Graham thought, how he had swept them along. He and Cheyney and Burns, with two other men whose names Graham had never heard, who had disappeared after the action, and whom Graham suspected of being unofficial actors from Cheyney's department, had immobilised Vishinsky's welcoming committee in ten minutes, and settled down to wait for that dreadful, dark moment on the beach when the Russian had died. Graham thought he would forever remember the terror and the realisation on the man's face and the way his body, almost cut in half by Cheyney's blast, was thrown back into the water and sprayed the torchlight with blood. He and Burns had taken the surrender of the other two, and it was only then that bedlam had broken loose, with the police, the Procurator Fiscal, the Chief Constable and the outrider, Pierce, grim, imperturbable, satisfied. And then they were off again in another fast car, searching out the last actor.

'What will you do after this, Peter?' said Cheyney.

'Go away,' said Graham in a tired voice. 'Take Maria and Tommy and some sick leave and go quietly away somewhere, and try to forget all this blood.'

'The boy's all right?'

'He will be. Whatever poison got into him it's gone – I mean moral poison, not the physical stuff. He's shaken, but that time at your place was very good for him. We talked a lot, you know, more than we've done for a long time. And now the three of us will go away.'

'Yes,' said Cheyney, his voice, too, suddenly weary. 'There's been too much blood and too much evil this time. Far too much.'

They drove along in a slightly stilted silence, down the long Fenland road at the end of which, so the map told them, they would find, isolated, the last refuge listed in Mr Quex's address book. Graham's heart and confidence were failing him: they had been remarkably lucky so far, but he no longer believed Quex was to be found in this lair. Cheyney was speaking aloud, quietly, almost to himself.

'Yes. There's been too much blood. Albert, Charlie, Grey, Vishinsky and Nelson. God knows what happened in that house. I'm so terribly tired of it all.'

Then he stiffened. 'Ah. There it is.'

They had come over a sudden hump in the road, and saw at its end the gate of an ample-sized bungalow, painted green and fronted by a small, absolutely plain, lawn. Behind the house stretched the dank fens, desolate in the cold autumn afternoon. And the door of the house was open; and there was no way of concealing their approach.

'The bird has flown,' said Graham.

'Well, go carefully all the same,' said Cheyney.

They left the car a few yards from the gate and, with it for protection, inspected the house. 'Cover me,' said Cheyney. The heavy Mauser in his hand, he went for the gate at a run, jumped it, hit the lawn on the other side, rolled, and was at the open door of the house. There had been neither response nor movement.

Seconds later, Graham followed him.

They found Quex in the large studio-style living-room of the bungalow, and Graham flinched at the man's obesity. He was sitting in a huge armchair, Lavinia Dawson, snarling in fear, on a footstool at his feet. He was unarmed, unshaven, unkempt and his eyes were glassy. There seemed no-one but himself in the house.

Cheyney signalled and Graham went rapidly from room to room of the bungalow, kicking open each door, following through at speed: but this was a house deserted. The only furnished room, it seemed, was the one in which they had found Quex. He returned there and reported. Quex and Cheyney, it appeared, had not spoken in his absence: Cheyney just stood there, tall and straight, his gun trained on the fat man.

Then he said, in a very gentle voice: 'Lavinia, go and wait in the car.'

She was as dishevelled and untidy as her master, her face dirty and frightened. Then Quex said, in a voice as gentle as Cheyney's, 'Go, Lavinia,' and she went, sliding past them in the doorway and then running.

'Well,' said Quex, with something of a return to his old manner, 'you have managed to do for me, my dear Colonel Cheyney, and now you have taken me. I could hardly' – this with the dreadful chuckle that seemed to take time to travel all the way from his groin to his throat – 'have disguised myself and fled the country, could I? When Vishinsky did not report I knew what had happened and came to this little hidy-hole to await you.'

Cheyney asked the question which gave him his last triumph, and vindicated his reading of Quex.

'You did not disband your people?'

'Oh dear me no. If their master was to go down it was right – essential – that they go down too. Mr Pierce will find it all intact. I presume you do have my papers?'

Cheyney nodded.

Quex said, 'My greatest mistake. I misread you, but,' and his eyes blazed, 'my trial will be a great one,' he proclaimed, his high voice rising with intensity, every part of his flesh quivering, a hand raised to point at Cheyney. 'It will last for a year and I will die in its course. But I will leave to my beloved country a monument of terror. My speech from the dock will go on for days and I will strike fear and destruction into all hearts. You, you puny middle-aged fool, you do not realise the strength of my heritage, it will be proclaimed . . .'

'There will be no trial.'

For a moment Quex did not hear Cheyney. Then he stopped. His mouth was open, revealing the pink cavern inside. Saliva ran from either corner down his jowls, over his meagre, dirty stubble, and on to his grimy shirt front. Unfocused eyes slowly fixed themselves on Cheyney. The right hand flapped in the air.

'This is the creature who tried to destroy your boy, Peter – settle it.'

Graham advanced and levelled his gun. Quex's eyes had gone out of focus again. His huge chest was labouring, both hands – those tiny, neat, almost boneless hands, now begrimed – scrabbled ineffectively at his shirt. His breathing was so short and strained that it seemed he would die as he sat. He tried to speak. Nothing came but spittle. Quex, so powerful forty-eight hours ago, was turned suddenly into a gross, helpless, wreck. A heaving, choking, almost inhuman mass, unable to gain comfort or purchase anywhere in the chair.

'Allen,' whispered Graham in horror, 'I ... I can't do it.'

Colonel Cheyney's gun boomed once.